MY

BROTHER

ANDRÉS

*AN INSPIRATIONAL YOUNG ADULT COMING-OF-AGE NOVEL
SET IN TURBULENT MEXICO IN 1968*

PETER PURCHASE

DUNE
PUBLISHING

Perth Western Australia

First published in Australia 2024 by Dune Publishing
Copyright © Peter Purchase 2024 www.peterpurchasebooks.com

My Brother Andrés

Cataloguing-in-Publication data is available from
The National Library of Australia

General acknowledgement is made to the following for permission
to reprint previously published material: Courtesy various artists
and other sources held on Alamy and Shutterstock used for chapter
heading photos.

ISBN: 978-0-9756216-2-2 (paperback)
          978-0-9756216-3-9 (epub)

Cover photograph: A view of Urique from Cerocahui in the Copper
Canyon, in the Sierra Madre Mountains, north-west Mexico -
(courtesy Prisma Dukas – Alamy stock photo).

*For those who died in the Tlatelolco massacre
in Mexico City on 2 October 1968.*

Aqui esta mi secreto.
Es muy simple: soló con el corazón se puede ver correctamente;
Lo que es esenciel es invisible a los ojos.

And now here is my secret. It's very simple: it's only with the heart that one can see rightly; what is essential is invisible to the eye.

Antoine de Saint-Exupéry

The Little Prince, April 1943

Alicia in a thoughtful mood – Courtesy Carlos Neri / Alamy stock photo

PROLOGUE

IT IS MY EIGHTEENTH birthday, April 17, 1978, late in the afternoon. My brother Andrés and I are on the balcony of his third storey unit in Mazatlán, Mexico, gazing down towards the city spread below us and the Pacific Ocean beyond.

The air is still, and the sun is about to sink beneath the western horizon, painting the sky in swathes of scarlet and orange. We can still make out the silhouettes of Wolf, Deer and Bird Islands across the shimmering sea.

We can see the sports stadium and the long stretch of the Malecon seafront promenade from up here. It's Andrés's favourite running track, beside the ocean.

Ten years older than me, he's been testing the latest prosthetic foot for running sent to him by the Ottobock Company in Germany. He is one of a team of athletes selected from around the world to use the latest prosthetics. He is as determined as ever to compete in a Paralympic Games wearing one, even if he has to wait until the year 2000 for the International Olympic Committee to accept prosthetics.

He'll be fifty years old by then, but we both have Tarahumaran Indian blood in us. We're among the best long-distance runners in the world, matching the East Africans.

That's why we call ourselves the Rarámurí, the light-footed ones, who run across the ridges and the slopes of the Copper Canyon in the Sierra Madre Mountains.

We spent this morning running along the Malecon, the sea breeze cooling us and the rich salty smell of the sea giving us the energy for an occasional sprint between the lamposts.

I've been here now for a week.

I've graduated from Saucillo High at last. I'm about to enrol at the Guadalajara University. I decided to study Languages and Applied Linguistics there. It was an easy decision. I already speak four languages: Tarahumaran and Spanish fluently and English and French a little. Besides, I hated Maths and was only moderately interested in Science. I left all that to Andrés, who was good at both. Especially Architecture, which is his day job in Mazatlán.

It's hard to believe I've left school after so many years. Looking back, it seems time has flown, whereas before I graduated time seemed to drag on forever.

Andrés grins at me and says, "So, Alicia, this time in August you'll be a university student."

"At last. Another four months. It's taken long enough."

"It has, and the University will test you. How you face the challenges will tell us who you are. How determined."

How I face the challenges? I wonder. *How determined I am? That's always been at the heart of my story.*

As he speaks, the years fall away. I see myself once again a terrified girl of eight, standing on the bloodstained paving stones of the Tlatelolco Plaza in Mexico City in October 1968. Deafened by the gunfire and horrified by the bodies falling around me, I will myself to take the last shots in my camera before I run. Then I sprint to safety from the massacre through the labyrinth of the Aztec ruins beside the plaza.

It is a self-defining moment when I bravely held my ground.

The memory will never leave me.

While I'm in Mazatlán I intend to write our story as I remember it.

I've brought my typewriter and made a start yesterday.

I've decided to call it *My Brother Andrés*.

Enjoy.

Sunflowers on Mothers Day – Courtesy Shutterstock

CHAPTER ONE

1

In Cerocahui, beside the Copper Canyon in Northwestern Mexico, May 1967

MY MOTHER, SURÉ, DIED on 10 May 1960, a month after I was born.

I can't remember her, but I've spent my life trying to recall her.

Her particular smell.

Her comforting touch.

The beating of her heart against my own.

I have a photograph showing me feeding at her right breast, taken a week before she died. I carry it with me everywhere. She held me in her arms for those thirty days. I treasure every moment of what I imagine was our closeness.

The day she died is Mother's Day, of all days. Can you believe it?

When I was growing up and missing her, my father, Victor, used to tell me the date proved I was so special Mamá made it her purpose in life to give birth to me, despite the risks.

She was forty years old.

He'd take me in his arms and give me a consoling embrace, often cradling my face in his hands—but in the secret corner of my mind, I'd wish it was Mamá comforting me.

I'd feel confused and even more upset, and guilty too, for hurting Papá if he ever found out how I felt.

Every year without fail, we used to visit Mamá's older sister, my *Tía* Ariché, on the anniversary of Mamá's death. We'd spend a week at her home in Cerocahui. It was deep in the Sierra Madre Mountains among the canyons. There we would honour Mamá's memory as though we were celebrating the *Día de los Muertos*, the Day of the Dead, six months early.

2

The first such visit I clearly remember occurred in May, 1967.

I was seven years old.

We drove up from our home in Saucillo the day before, in my Tarahumaran grandfather Cerrildo's 1956 Golden Hawk Studebaker. It was a seven-hour journey, with short stopovers in Cuauhtemoc and Creel.

My older brother Andrés let me win four games of checkers out of seven during the drive. "Because you're still a beginner and learning the moves," he told me.

I read Andrés's latest comics between games.

I enjoyed reading and rereading the adventures of my favourite superhero, Kalimán, and his eleven-year-old apprentice, Solín.

That is, until I was car sick—just the once and fortunately outside the car. Papá bent me over, an arm around my waist and his free hand holding back my hair.

"Try not to soil my shoes," he kept urging me.

I slept the rest of the trip stretched out on the back seat with my feet up on Andrés's lap.

The next morning I woke up early.

I found my *Tía* Ariché sitting in silence on the chilly patio, looking out across her grapevines.

Andrés was out on his early morning training run, and Papá and Abu Cerrildo were still asleep.

Tía's excitable white miniature Schnauzers, Zipi and Zape, lay alert beside her. They had their muzzles on their paws. They were scanning the vineyard for any thick-billed green parrots or other birds daring to feed on the grapes.

When I sat down, Zape lifted his overhanging eyebrows and met my gaze. The glint of warning in his bright, dark eyes let me know he'd nip me if I got too close. I promptly lifted my bare feet to the seat of my chair and rested my chin on my raised knees. I wrapped my arms around them, and he dismissed me and resumed his watch.

The green and gold leaves of the vines gleamed as the sun rose behind us. Clouds of tiny midges shimmered here and there in particles of light above the ripening purple bunches.

The sun's rays slanting towards the rim of the Urique Canyon warmed my back and shoulders. It melted away my icy dread at the thought of bothering Tía with the question I'd asked Papá and Abu Cerrildo countless times.

"Tía, please tell me the truth this time."

No one else will and I'm sick of asking, the thought ran through my mind.

"What truth, sweetheart?"

"What happened to Mamá? Why did she die?"

Until now, Papá and Abu Cerrildo have avoided answering. You're too young to understand. You hardly knew her, if at all. All in good time. As if the cause of her death is a secret. Or they don't want to upset me by discovering something unbearable in her passing.

Tía's shrewd black eyes stared thoughtfully into mine for several long moments. She rearranged a loose strand of her thick black hair streaked with grey back into the bun coiled on top of her head.

I took a deep, determined breath.

I held her narrow-eyed look, unsure what she was thinking or what was coming next. She slowly nodded, rocking her body from the waist up in her creaky wicker chair. The gold Aztec Tree of Life pendant on her necklace swung like a hypnotic pendulum across her black, loose-fitting linen blouse.

"Your Mamá got really sick, Alicia," she said at last.

Her voice was an unexpected hiss. "It was septicaemia. After an emergency operation to bring you into the world."

To bring me into the world?

I was unsure what she meant. Her words struck me like an accusation. I ducked my head as though she'd slapped me.

After a long pause, relaxing back in her chair, she continued, "You are seven years old, going on seventeen. It's time you knew yours was a complicated breech birth. It took so much longer than we expected. It was never-ending and very painful for her. *Pero ella era estoica*, but she was very brave."

Puzzled, I looked up and stared at her defiantly as she gathered her thoughts.

Was it my fault, after all?

Then my stubbornness gave way. I nodded, pretending with a thoughtful look that I understood her. She reached across to pat my shoulder as if she understood my confusion.

"You arrived feet first. We couldn't turn you round," she said.

She raised her eyebrows and showed her strong white teeth in a smile I guessed was sympathetic. Her voice was suddenly reassuring and matter of fact.

"It seemed to us as if you couldn't wait to meet the ground running. *Como la pequeña cabra montañosa*, like the little mountain goat you've become. But Suré had just turned forty.

That's a very dangerous age to have a child. Especially for a Tarahumaran Indian woman."

She leaned forward, wrapped her arms around me and squeezed.

"And even though the pregnancy was unplanned," she went on, "she wouldn't listen to our advice. As usual. An abortion? No. She was having none of it."

She gave a quick shake of her head. "She was determined to have you, *mijita*. She always was the pig-headed one. Just like you. And the prettiest."

Before I could wriggle away, she said, "We wouldn't have it any other way, honey. She did us all a favour. You, especially you."

Her smell was earthy and her voice vibrated as she spoke beside my ear.

When I broke free and ran, I heard her call out. 'Relax, *nenita*, relax, child. Now her spirit is *kiri-i-kiri huko*. At peace."

She cackled as if to emphasise the Tarahumaran phrase she'd shouted. One of the working mules in the paddock beside the house brayed in response.

They were both silenced as the door slammed behind me.

The words she yelled again were faint, 'At peace, compared to the rest of us… me and you both.'

It took me many years to realise I was partly responsible for Mamá's agonising death and understand that she'd considered an abortion early in her pregnancy but decided against it.

Even Tía Ariché, who hadn't realised she'd be fostering me when Mamá died, advised her to abort me.

Almost, but not quite.

My life in exchange for hers.

Was that to be my ongoing story?

$\mathscr{3}$

When I opened the curtains an hour later, Tía was still sitting alone.

The sun was firing up the blood-red roses blooming on the trellis above her head.

A pine-scented breeze brushed across the vineyard. Its minty fragrance reached me through the open window. And there, beyond the nearby shadows of the canyons and the mauve silhouettes of distant mountains, I saw the pale three-quarter moon hanging like a fingernail in the brightening sky.

"What colour would you paint it, Mamá?" I whispered.

I pictured us standing together at the window admiring the landscape. I'd started fantasising about us doing so back at home in Saucillo, allowing her to share with me all the experiences she'd missed.

"*Oh, something golden, mijita, with the sun coming up,*" I imagined her saying. "*Something golden would be perfect.*"

The fact that I was imagining her speaking and putting words in her mouth did not make our shared moment any less real to me. It seemed to me to add to it.

Before rejoining Tía, I took out Mamá's treasured brown leather beret from my chest of drawers. Papá gave it to me a month ago on my latest birthday. He also gave me another two of her favourite things—a silver butterfly brooch embedded with garnet stones green as emeralds and a fringed sky-blue silk rebozo shawl he told me she'd used as a child.

Before she died, she'd insisted I should have them when I was old enough.

She didn't want them buried with her in the coffin.

I hadn't yet worn any of them.

I'd been afraid to.

And now I wasn't sure I deserved to.

I braced myself, put both hands inside the beret, held it open and placed it over my head. I tugged at my ponytail to adjust the beret there before tightening the leather thong running around the rim, so it fitted me perfectly.

I stood for several minutes facing the mirror. I arranged the beret so that the bright green oak tree emblem on it was front and centre.

It's shaped just like Tía's Tree of Life, I thought. *This is how Mamá must have worn it. She would have checked her reflection as she adjusted it, just as I am.*

I felt strangely connected to Mamá at that moment.

I could not remember her, but now perhaps I could get to know her by piecing together everything I was told about her. I'd allow my imagination to do the rest.

Perhaps.

It was a start.

What I wanted then more than anything was to have used the superpowers I'd learned from Kalimán and done a somersault in Mamá's womb seven years ago. Then I'd move headfirst down her birth canal, leaving us both alive and well when I was born.

A surge of relief, almost of happiness, ran through me.

The painful, unsettling sense of loneliness I usually experienced when I asked or thought about her fell away.

I smiled at my image, as though her eyes were looking into mine and mine hers—and the unexpected idea flashed across my mind—*This is how I'd feel if Mamá was giving me the love I need to give myself.*

On my way out through the dining room, I surprised myself—I used my fingertips to transfer a kiss to Mamá's charcoal portrait.

It had been sketched when she was young, long before she became my mamá. Up till then I'd always thought it was the face of a stranger.

For the first time now, I recognised myself in her.

The high cheekbones with their shadows, though mine were not yet as full.

The wide-set eyes. The hint of creases at the edges of her smile.

The picture was propped up on the temporary *ofrenda* altar the maid Ofelia and I helped Tía construct the day before, to commemorate Mamá's death. It held a glass of water for her, and a bowl of her favourite salted cashews and peanuts.

Ofelia had lit five candles and incense sticks earlier for the day. The brightly coloured wreath of crepe paper flowers we'd made matched the two vases of brilliant orange and yellow marigolds I'd picked. I found them in the rows bordering the vegetable garden. We believed their strong musky scent would guide Mamá's spirit on her journey home to protect us, or away to the other world awaiting her.

Surrounding the offerings, Ofelia laid a semi-circle of her magic stones and crystals—a miniature wall to protect Mamá from evil spirits and other *diablitos* who might want to cause her harm. Standing guard at the entrance was a small white *calavera* sugar skull Ofelia made. She decorated it with rainbow-coloured icing and sequins.

A copy of Filippino Lippi's *Adoration of the Magi* was hanging on the wall beside the altar. It was one of Tía Ariché's favourite religious illustrations. She believed it guaranteed Mamá good fortune in the afterlife.

When I walked out, Tía Ariché adjusted the empty wicker chair beside her without facing me. She patted the seat.

"Are you hungry, *mijita?*" she asked. "After breakfast why don't we ride the horses down to Urique? We can leave some flowers on your mamá's grave like we did last year.

Would you like that?"

She looked at me with her eyebrows raised, waiting for me to nod.

"I know Suré would," she went on. "*Nada mas segura*, nothing surer. What do you say? Some sunflowers again? Her favourites. Why don't you go and pick some? We can stay there overnight and come back up tomorrow. Oh, I like your beret. It really suits you. You look as lovely in it as your mamá did."

I looked away.

A warm glow rushed through me at her compliment, especially when she mentioned my similarity to Mamá.

When I stood to get the clippers, Andrés appeared on the path leading to the canyon edge. He had removed his t-shirt and wrapped it around his head against the sun. The dark skin of his chest gleamed above his faded blue running shorts.

His black mixed-breed Calupoh dog, Geronimo, looking like greyhound with a white flash down his chest, bounded past him. His long tongue was extended and his tail wagged madly when he recognised me. He slurped at his water bowl before slumping with a heavy sigh beneath the table. He stretched out, panting, just beyond kicking distance of Tía's sandalled feet and a respectable distance from Zipi and Zape when they gave him a combined warning growl.

Andrés glided up to us.

He was barely panting.

He looked as though he hadn't raised a sweat.

He placed his metre-long snake-catching pole on the table and pressed the button on the stopwatch he wore on his left wrist.

He was ten years older than me at seventeen, and I worshipped the ground he ran on. I used to join him, running for short stretches whenever he'd let me.

In spite of our teasing, he insisted he was training for the 1968 Olympics in Mexico City. They were now a year away.

He'd been training for it ever since I'd known him.

"*Una hora y veinte*, an hour and twenty," he said. "Same as yesterday. Halfway down to Lorenzo's lookout and back." He glanced at me. "You should have joined me, lazybones." Then he noticed the beret. "Or should I call you Che Guevara? All you need is his red star… and his beard."

"I'm not a lazybones and I'm not Che, I'm *me*. Come with us to Urique after breakfast and I'll show you who can run."

"I'll have a shower and breakfast first. Then we'll find out who shows who."

As he walked away, I was reminded how much we looked alike, how closely we shared our looks with Mamá.

A thrill ran through me.

It gave me a new sense of belonging; a deep connection I was craving to offset the aloneness I sometimes experienced when I was mixing with girls my age who had their mothers.

5

Hours later, we laid the sunflowers across Mamá's horizontal ochre-painted grave in the Urique cemetery. It lay in the shade of an alder tree.

"*Los girasoles simbolizan la adoración*," Tía said. "Sunflowers symbolise adoration, as I told you last time."

She squinted up through the leaves at the pale blue sun-scorched afternoon sky.

"They may not last long in this heat, but our adoration will." She hesitated, before adding, "*Mientras Dios esté feliz de sonreírnos.* For as long as God is happy to smile down on us."

We paid our respects and left offerings of food and drink Tía had prepared. We arranged them on the grave.

We stood with bowed heads for a minute before Tía murmured, "Alright, you two can run now."

Andrés and I chased each other in and out of the white-trunked sycamore trees encircling the cemetery. The trees were so pale and ghostly Andrés partly convinced me as we ran that they came out of the ground at the full moon and danced among the tombstones on their roots to the hooting of the giant owl roosting in their branches.

"That owl is La Lechuza," he said as we ran.

That was so unexpected I felt my skin freeze and goosebumps rush across my arms, the fine hairs on my forearms standing up.

I knew the myth. La Lechuza was the shape-shifting wicked old witch who turned into an owl and swooped down, her claws drawn, to seize unsuspecting children at night. She ripped them into pieces with her beak as she took revenge on people who'd wronged her.

The goosebumps eased when he suggested Mamá was running unseen beside us.

"She loved to run with me when she was alive," he said.

Suddenly I could sense her there.

The eerie rustling of the breeze among the sycamore leaves was no longer the beating of a giant owl's wings but the whisper of Mamá's breathing.

It was a sound so soothing that in that moment it struck me Mamá was not dead to us.

I felt a rush of emotion.

I took his hand and squeezed it.

He must be missing Mamá as much as I am, I realised.

He allowed me to hold it for several privileged moments before releasing mine to sprint the last few metres to the gravesite.

6

Later, we sat for some time in the nearby chapel of Our Lady of Guadalupe. The cool, calm silence of the chapel was occasionally shattered by the expanding corrugated iron roof cracking like a starter's pistol.

Tía reminded us to make the sign of the cross and kneel when we entered.

As I did so, I looked up at the mural of the dark-skinned Madonna painted on the wall behind the altar.

She was still wearing the bright purple eyepatch someone crudely painted over her right eye during the Easter celebrations last year. It protected her from witnessing the suffering of her son Jesus on the cross, but allowed her to watch through her left eye the destruction and burning in hell of the papier mâché effigy of the traitor Judas. That was the climax of the ceremonies.

Before she settled into a pew, Tía Ariché adjusted her favourite cotton rebozo shawl embroidered in olive-green and gold snakeskin diamonds over her head and shoulders.

Next, she removed my beret. She replaced it with Mamá's rebozo. Then she told me I looked as fresh and untouched as the Virgin Mary herself wearing it.

"So did your mamá when she was your age and as innocent," she added as she adjusted it. Then she leaned forward, gave me a meaningful glance and said, *"Pero sin tu rebeldía,* Alicia. But without your rebelliousness."

My rebelliousness? How dare you? You're not my mother. You never will be!

I forced a smile and bit my tongue, but I'm sure my eyes gave me away.

For a brief second, I sent her a spark of defiance.

It didn't last, though. I had too much respect and fear for her uncertain temper.

"Oh, look at you, *mijita*. So fiery. So headstrong." She shook her head. "What are we to do with you?"

Then her expression softened and her voice changed.

She reminded us that Mamá was far from dead and we should pray for her. Still alive in that other place, with spiritual access to our world, she was no doubt watching over us.

"A miracle, thanks be to God. Nothing more," she said.

Part of me wanted to believe her, and did, but in the following silence, perplexing questions flooded my mind.

Has Mamá forgiven me without me asking her to because she loves me and is my mother? Am I worthy of her sacrifice? Does she miss me as much as I miss her? Can I ever make it up to her? And the question tormenting me above all: *If giving me life meant she'd died in accordance with some miraculous purpose, as Papá had suggested, what does it mean for my future? A future I was destined to spend without her.*

"A miracle?" I asked.

"A miracle for certain, just as you are."

She patted my knee.

She gave me her familiar inscrutable smile and contradictory look. "On the other hand, only God truly knows."

"And if God has his doubts, then we keep guessing?" Andrés broke in.

"Sssssssssssst! Not in this place," Tía Ariché scolded him.

She stretched across my back and delivered a sharp slap to the back of his head.

"You leave your doubts at the door, Andrés! And any other disbelief you've got floating around in your empty skull. In this place, our faith keeps hope alive, not questioned by your so-called logic and reason."

I suppressed a laugh when I heard him grumble as he flinched.

"*Si. Si.* Okay, Tía."

He made a face.

Then I heard him murmur under his breath, "*Pero no,* but no," as he often did, reasserting his seventeen-year-old Mexican manliness.

When we left the chapel, Andrés asked if we could race along the thousand-metre sandy circuit cleared of rocks beside the river.

"We don't have time," Tía replied. "It's getting late."

Impulsively ignoring her, I took off my riding boots. I laced on my made-to-measure huaraches. They'd been designed for running—with car tyre soles.

"Race you up the hill!" I shouted, and with a head start, I sprinted with Andrés and Geronimo over the rocks and slippery gravel up the slope to the tethered horses.

I punched him several times on the arm when he said he'd let me win.

"Tía's right about your running." He gazed intently at me, his dark brown eyes alight. "You are a little mountain goat—and you look like one."

"That makes two of us," my tongue surprised me by replying before I'd thought of an answer, "and you're ten years older than me so you must be twice as ugly."

My quick response caught him off-guard.

"*Tienes razón.* Well said!" he exclaimed, and we both laughed till the tears came,

He tickled my ribs with the bony fingers of his left hand, while he held my upper arm with his right. He was careful to protect the long fingernails he'd grown for Papá and his good friend Tío Guillermo, who were teaching him to play new flamenco techniques on his guitar.

Of course I'd grown mine as well. When Andrés was practising after his lessons, he allowed me to sit beside him, joyfully tinkering with the child-size guitar Papá gave me when I complained about being left out.

Tía Ariché, beaming, struggled up the hill towards us. I could see her wondering what the fuss was all about. The two rebozos lay across her shoulders and in her right hand she held the little *hielera* cooler with our Lulú drinks on ice.

When she lifted the lid, she surprised us with an unexpected extra treat—a slice of her homemade *mazapan de cacahuate*, her peanut marzipan. It was left over from the plateful of pieces she'd placed on Mamá's grave, along with the paper cup of her favourite drink—crushed-ice mango licuado.

Before she handed us our rewards, she held out her arms, as always.

"*Abrázame*, hug me," she said.

And I did, just as I'd have hugged Mamá if she'd lived.

The smoky smell of sweat and camphor lingered when she let me go and I asked myself achingly, *Did Mamá feel and smell the same?*

7

In Mazatlán, Mexico, April 1978

Looking back on it now that I'm eighteen, when I was seated between Tía Ariché and Andrés in the chapel, her dark Tarahumaran skin and his deep Mexican tan so distinctly contrasted to my paler fawn, I felt different.

In some way blessed.

And yet the same.

I sensed confusing emotions stirring within me I didn't yet understand.

For the first time, I feared living in a mystifying world where I suspected my destiny was no longer of my choosing or my will, but more a matter of chance.

I learned on that Mother's Day that the world, despite its magic and captivating beauty, can turn and strike you quicker than a homeless cat you're stroking in the street when it rubs against your leg. Shocked and bleeding, you stifle your scream and wonder, *Did I deserve the vicious clawing and the unexpected bite?*

And if so, why?

Either way, you carry the scars as a lifelong reminder of your questions and the lessons you learn.

And the confusing thought struck me, *If my relationship with Mamá—the most important of my life—lasted no longer than a month, are all my relationships only temporary and destined to end quickly?*

When we returned to Cerocahui the next day, Tía took me out to one of the garden sheds. It was dark inside, the single cobwebbed window grimy. She reached up to a shelf where there was a row of lidded jars.

"Cup your hands together," she said.

She shook the jar, unscrewed the rusty lid with some effort and poured a handful of small white sunflower seeds into my open palms. "Now go, *mijita*. You know where to plant them. The early ones will be ready for you next year."

Since then, I've taken a handful of seeds to plant in whatever flowerbeds are available wherever I am. That way I'll have a bunch of sunflowers in full bloom on the following Mother's Day.

Caring for them as they grow, watching their buds develop and listening to stories told about Mamá as I grew up, have extended the one unremembered month we shared into years.

It gives me a comforting, imaginary sense of bonding with the mother I never knew.

One day I'll be as old as she was when she died.

That thought gives me an intense, uneasy awareness of my mortality, as if I'm living on borrowed time. And it reminds me—just as the growing sunflowers do each year—that mourning for her will never end.

What I learned that day I spent with Tía Ariché I've never forgotten.

I've often returned to those moments for insights into my story, my coming of age and my quest for self-awareness, to better understand who I am and accept the person I've become.

There I am, my eager younger self, thrilled Tía has confirmed I looked so much like Mamá when she was younger, wearing her beret and rebozo and listening for further observations to add to my growing picture of her.

She took her stories with her when she died.

Listening to Tía enabled me to imagine her retelling them.

There are times when I remember Tía describe the challenges Mamá dealt with during my birth and explain how she faced her demons with the courage, determination and resolute independence I like to think I've inherited.

The bombing of Guernica – Courtesy the Chronicle / Alamy stock photos

CHAPTER TWO

1

In Saucillo, Northern Mexico, April 1968

ANOTHER MEANINGFUL MEMORY HAPPENED when Papá showed us his blue reinforced cardboard suitcase for the first time.

I had just turned eight years old.

I clearly remember him revealing the contents to us as he explained how he travelled alone from Spain to Mexico during the Spanish Civil War.

Andrés and I found him that day relaxed in his black leather armchair in the lounge. He was reading. He had his legs outstretched on a footstool, when we burst in from the garden.

We'd been sprinting around the circuit in the backyard of Papá's house in Saucillo. Abu Cerrildo had been coaching us, and we were heading to the kitchen for a drink.

Andrés skidded to a halt beside him.

"Papá, *por favor*, please tell us how you and Mamá met," he said.

Papá looked up.

He closed his book and retrieved his distance glasses from his forehead. He put them on, sat motionless for a second. Then he raised his eyebrows.

"*Again?*" he asked.

"Yes, again. *Por favor.*"

"I've told you before. We met on the cathedral steps in Chihuahua City. We were both nineteen and members of the Children's Cultural Army. Teaching illiterate kids and adults to read and write."

He rubbed his forehead as if to clear the horizontal furrows and allowed me to lift his feet from the footstool.

I made myself comfortable on it. I looked up at his long, thin sunburned face with its bony cheeks and a straight, high-bridged nose. I considered him more handsome than any cowboy in a Western on TV, especially considering his remarkable eyes. They were the same amber colour as mine, though in his you could see flecks of gold around the pupils when the light was bright.

I leant forward with my elbows on my knees, my chin on my hands and stared into them.

"I joined Mamá's group that day," he went on, before frowning for a moment as if collecting his thoughts. "Later, we played chess during the breaks at school. We used a set Abu Cerrildo carved for her."

"Like he does now? Using crystals from the Cave of Swords at the Naica mine?" I asked, picturing Abu at his workbench in the back garden, bent over his drills and cutting equipment as he shaped the pieces, peering through his jeweller's eyepiece now and then.

"The same."

"And you liked her when you both played chess?"

"Yes, I did. We fell in love. You want me to go on?"

"That's not what I asked," Andrés said. "I want to know what happened *before* you came to Mexico. Before you met her. You've never told us the story. Not in full, anyway."

"Because it's such a long one."

"I want to know everything. Not just the bits and pieces you've told us so far."

"Every detail?" He pointed at Andrés and shook his forefinger. "You don't know what you're asking."

"Yes, I do. It's our story too, don't forget."

Persistent as always, Andrés held both hands out, palms up, his eyebrows deliberately raised. I knew that stubborn look and smiled to myself. *He won't give in. Not now. Not ever.*

"Your story will help Alicia and me understand," he insisted.

"Understand?"

"What you were like as a boy. How you came to *be* in Chihuahua City. Besides..." he seemed to search for the words, "we want to know where *we* belong in the story. At least, I do."

"Me too," I said at once, supporting him as usual, but uncertain what he meant.

"Ah, I see." Papá nodded, frowning.

He rose abruptly to his feet and placed his open book face down on his chair. "Very well. Come with me."

We followed his tall, angular frame to the privacy of his darkened bedroom.

He pulled aside the curtains. Blazing sunlight filled the room.

He lifted down a blue suitcase I'd never seen before, concealed on top of his wardrobe. He placed it on the bed and dusted it off with the back of his hand. He flicked aside the rusty locks and slowly opened it, as though disclosing a mystery to us.

I was excited as he showed us the contents.

It seemed he was bringing his past into our present at last.

He was introducing us to the magic of his treasured boyhood memories lying in wait for us all our lives.

Peering over his shoulder, I glimpsed a plastic bag of chipped, multicoloured glass marbles and steel ball bearings, a pair of battered yoyos, and a chess set in a net bag. Its pieces were intricately carved in light and dark wood. I saw crayons and several sketching pads, and a pair of black leather running shoes, cracked and twisted out of shape, their long spikes rusty. Two large, beige celluloid Philip Morris cigar boxes stood out beside a handful of comics and magazines,

What surprising story is each item going to tell us? I wondered.

Beside them was a photo album.

He took out the album, placed it on his lap and moved the open suitcase to one side.

Then he invited us to sit beside him.

"My papá Xavier, your other grandfather, was a professional photographer in Spain," he said, opening the cover. "He was a freelance photojournalist and a Republican when the civil war broke out in 1936, over thirty years ago. He sold his pictures to the newspapers or to the highest bidder—whoever paid him enough to feed the family. Which wasn't often. During the war there were shortage,s and everything was rationed. We were almost starving."

3

He held the album open at the third page.

He put his hand with his fingers splayed over the photo on the right, keeping it hidden.

At the top of the left-hand page, written in neat white

cursive, I read the words *Gernika—antes*, Guernica—before. Beneath it the date—26 April 1937.

The black and white photo showed the peaceful scene of a small country town that could be anywhere in Spain or Mexico. It was taken at street level. I saw two and three-storey buildings with tiled roofs, arched front doors and whitewashed walls. They had windows framed with dark bricks and decorative cast iron grills. Cobbled streets led to an open square—a plaza filled with crowds of people sitting beneath the trees.

It had a bandstand in the centre.

There were some animals held in wood-fenced pens—a handful of wide-horned cattle, and sheep, some black and others white.

I leaned across and pointed at a flat-roofed single-storey building facing the square. Many groups of young children were playing in the courtyard.

"What's that?" I asked. "It looks like a school."

"It is. A Basque school, an *ikastola euskadi*. See the name over the archway? The authorities set them up in smaller towns like Guernica and Durango during the civil war. They moved as many children as they could into them. Away from the big cities like Bilbao and Madrid. To keep them safe from the fighting and the bombing."

"They look happy."

"They do. It looks like some of them are playing hide and seek. And you can see those three girls skipping, just like you do."

Beyond them all, the tower of a church rose above the shadowy peaks of distant hills. Its clock read two-thirty.

The windswept sky was streaked with clouds.

Papá then raised his hand and pointed at the second photo.

"By eight o'clock that night it looked like this," he said.

At the top of the page I read *Gernika—después*, Guernica—afterwards.

I couldn't believe it.

It was like an apocalypse.

I stared in horror at the shattered buildings, flames raging here and there beneath a cloud of thick black smoke. The burned and gory remains of body parts barely recognisable as animal or human lay scattered across piles of rubble beside many deep black bomb craters. Houses and their cellars lay blasted open, people who had sheltered in them buried alive.

And then I gasped at the flattened ruins of the school.

I was struck with such horror, my heartbeat faltered.

Are they all dead? Those poor children!

I looked away for a full minute, nauseated, fighting to calm myself and swallowing my tears to stop them, before glancing back.

The shadows of three firemen from a brigade unit stood pumping water ineffectively at the flames.

Fractured tubes the size of relay batons glinted in the blackened wreckage.

Andrés pointed them out. "What are they?"

"They're the aluminium shells of phosphorus grenades. The bigger ones are thermite bombs," Papá replied. "They were used to create a firestorm across the town. Imagine the damage, especially when the people or animals caught fire."

Papá told us the bombing had been carried out by German pilots of the Condor Legion flying the latest Heinkel bombers. They werre on loan from Hitler to General Franco's Nationalists.

Andrés stared at the two photographs, shaking his head. "Are they both Abu Xavier's photos?"

"They are. He showed them to me in Barcelona after he'd developed them."

"Was he there during the bombing?"

"The day after."

"And the first photo?"

"I'm not sure. He was working in Bilbao at the time, so he could have visited Guernica any day before the bombing."

"So it may not have been taken on the day before the bombing?"

"Knowing him, he'd have done everything to find a shot he'd taken as close to that date as possible. I remember one thing that really angered him. Some other world-famous photojournalists working in Spain *staged* the photographs they sent out for publication." He glanced at Andrés, frowning. "Prize winning photos, some of them. They looked real, but they weren't. They were posed many kilometres behind the front lines. They used actors dressed for the part, complete with cartridge belts and rifles. They were cheats, in other words."

"Why?"

"Because they couldn't get close enough to the fighting. Or were afraid. Or too lazy."

"How could they get away with it?"

"By blurring the background so the locations couldn't be verified. Your abuelo refused to do that. All his shots were genuine. He was the most honest man I know."

"Up to a thousand people were killed," he said. "We don't know the exact number. Guernica didn't just change world opinion against the Nationalists. It also changed my life forever."

"You came to Mexico?" Andrés asked.

"I did."

"So we owe Guernica our lives, Alicia and me?"

Papá closed the album. He spread both hands across the cover, smoothing it out.

"You could say so. When Abu Xavier saw the extent of the damage and took these photographs, he made up his mind to send me here. On my own. It happened as quickly as *that*." He snapped his fingers; the piercing click beside my ear made me jump.

"A month later, I boarded the steamship *Mexique* in France, in Bordeaux, with other selected children. We arrived in Veracruz in Mexico in early June."

"How old were you?" Andrés asked.

"Twelve."

"Did Abuela Marina or Abuelo Xavier see you off?"

"Mamá did. Your abuela Marina. She came to the França station the day I left."

He drummed his fingers on the photo album for several long moments before he broke the silence.

"I never saw her again."

He pursed his lips as the silence lengthened.

Never saw her again? Is she dead too, like Mamá? What is he remembering? It must be horrible, I thought,

And then, "You don't have to ask," he said. "She died at the battle of Ebro River a year later. In July. Papá told me in a letter."

"How?" Andrés asked.

Papá stared at Andrés.

Is he holding himself in check? He seems to be.

"All right," he said at last. "She was evacuating three wounded volunteers from Benifallet and the ambulance she was driving struck a mine. She's buried with them in the Rasquera cemetery in Tarragona. At least she had the dignity of a proper burial. Not a mass grave like many others."

Papá replaced the photo album in the suitcase and took out one of the beige cigar boxes.

He placed it on his lap.

He ran his fingertips over the two rearing lions facing off against each other in the logo embossed on the lid, as if he was reading them and its *veni vidi vici* motto—*I came, I saw, I conquered*—in braille.

He did not open it. He leant forward instead, placed it on the floor between his feet, and sat with his shoulders hunched.

And then, vigorously shaking his head, his fearful growl shattered the silence.

"*Guernica!* This takes me back, damn it!"

I jerked sideways and glanced up at him, alarmed.

Andrés placed a restraining hand on his forearm.

Papá looked at each of us in turn, then closed his eyes. He spread his arms across our shoulders and gradually tightened his grip, his fingers digging into my flesh until it hurt.

An icy foreboding rushed through me.

I twisted around and loosened his fingers, then held his hand in both of mine on my lap. A rush of empathy overtook me. About to cry, I began stroking the back of his hand, desperate to comfort him, but unsure how. When I looked up at his tormented face it blurred through my welling tears, and I looked away.

Thankfully, moments later, he relaxed. He opened his eyes, took a deep breath and gave us a quiet, knowing smile, the way he does. As if he'd decided.

"Very well," he said, "since you want my story, why don't I tell it to you? Where shall I start?"

"At the beginning," Andrés said.

"Very well. It's late in the afternoon in May 1937, during a thunderstorm in Barcelona. Imagine you're sitting beside me as you are now, in the little kitchen at the back of our house. My mamá, your abuela Marina, is opposite me. Your abuelo Xavier has just developed the photos of Guernica I've shown you. These two and four others. We watch him put them down one at a time on the mustard yellow plastic tablecloth. Face up.

In silence. He has just come home from Bilbao after months away at the front line, where the fighting was fierce. I have no idea what he's going to say, but his expression is so stern and the photos so shocking I know it's going to be terrible."

He held Andrés and me in suspense for a long moment before he told us what happened next.

His storytelling, as always, held us spellbound.

The Orphans of Morelia
- Courtesy Marco Enriquez / Mexican General National Archives

CHAPTER THREE

1

VICTOR: *In Barcelona, Spain, 6 May, 1937*

A STORM WAS RAGING with sudden bursts of thunder as deafening as gunfire, and the rain drumming against the kitchen windowpanes was so heavy we couldn't see through them.

I strained to catch what Papá was saying. He saw me frown and raised his voice to repeat what he'd said, but spoke so rapidly I still had trouble following him.

"I said we're sending you to Mexico, Victor. Either that or England."

It took me a moment to understand him. *Have I heard him correctly?* I wondered. Then his words struck me and I was horrified. Fear and confusion settled deep in my chest like a block of ice.

I reared back in my chair.

"What? *Me?* Going to Mexico?"

"It's either that or England, France or the Soviet Union. You speak very little French and no English or Russian, so Mexico where they speak Spanish is the obvious country to send you to."

"Why?" My mouth went dry, and my voice was shaking so much I could hardly speak.

He pointed at the six photographs he'd just developed, spread across the tablecloth. Then he rapped one of them with the knuckles of his right fist several times. He had selected the one that showed the bombed town of Guernica in ruins, with flames erupting everywhere.

"*Sobran las palabras!*" he growled. His face suddenly flushed and his eyes were so wild it shocked me. It wasn't like him. He was usually so calm. "Words can't express it. This picture speaks for itself," he said.

My mother Marina was sitting at the table opposite me. I'd been helping her with the baking. The rich yeasty smell of hot bread filled the kitchen. It would be the first loaf we'd had in a month. The shops were empty and rationing was strict.

I looked at her, begging for an explanation. She reached out and put her hand on mine to calm me. I was grateful, but still apprehensive.

"We're depending on you to put your best foot forward," Papá told me. "The President of Mexico, Lázaro Cárdenas, is setting up a special school for the refugee children in a city called Morelia, where he lives. He will be taking a special interest in the school. That will work to your advantage if you're selected."

Papá scooped the photos up and looked across at me.

"I've added your name to those going next month," he said. "The steamship *Mexique* will be sailing from Bordeaux for Veracruz on the twenty-sixth of May. If it's full, there are places still available aboard the *Habana*, leaving the Santurtzi docks in Bilbao for Southampton on the twenty-first. Mexico or England. Either way, you are going. Mamá and I agree on this. I'm sorry. We have no choice."

Mamá agrees with you? As soon as the words left his mouth I wished I hadn't heard them.

His warning frown and quick shake of his head as our eyes met discouraged me from interrupting him. "It's for your own good, Victor. You're twelve years old. We will not have you sent to the front when you turn thirteen in July or *Dios no lo quiera*, God forbid, fighting in Madrid."

He sat back, placed the stack of photos on the table and crossed his arms.

"On my own?" I stammered.

"Yes," Papá said.

Tense and breathless, I felt the world fall away beneath my feet. "For how long?"

Mamá held my right hand in both of hers. "Until the situation here is sorted out and things return to normal," she said quietly.

"How long will that take?"

"*Quién sabe*, who knows? A year? Two?"

"Can't you come with me?"

"No," Papá said. "Mamá is needed here to drive her ambulance."

"Two years?" My eyes filled with tears I couldn't stop. My throat was so tense I had to swallow. "*Two years!*"

"Possibly. I will not lie to you."

Papá placed the photograph of the ruins back on the table. He tapped it with his forefinger.

"I've told you before, General Franco and the Nationals are being assisted by Germany's Hitler and Italy's Mussolini. They're using the civil war to test their latest weapons. I hate to say so, but the Nationalists might win. We Republicans have the heart and the determination for a fight, but without the firepower, we're losing. The weapons Russia and Mexico are sending us don't match theirs." He shook his head. "It's another case of might is right, in which case we could become the unlucky losers who deserved to win."

"How will I contact you?" I asked, my voice still shaking as an unbearable feeling of helplessness seemed to paralyse me.

"All in good time," Papá said. "Arrangements will be made."

"Can't I stay here in Barcelona with you?"

"You risk being handed a rifle and sent where the fighting is."

"Others my age have done it. Even younger."

"Yes, and come back dead or mutilated in the back of ambulances. Ask Mamá. She has seen them. I will not risk it. In Mexico, you'll have a future. They are setting up that special school I mentioned, for all the children selected to go. As I said, the President of Mexico himself lives there and he'll be taking an interest in the children and the school. You can finish your education there if you're fortunate enough to be accepted for the voyage. Perhaps start a profession. In geology, maybe? I know you're interested—look at your rock collection—and you have the talent and the persistence for the study."

He stared at me, then added forcefully, "Remember what I've always drummed into you. *Serás exitoso siempre que aproveche al máximo sus oportunidades*, you will succeed, as long as you make the most of your opportunities and don't waste them. Set your goals and work hard to achieve them, one step at a time."

I was shocked.

I stared at him, not sure how to reply at first, taking in everything he'd just said and hardly believing what I was hearing. And then, "Finish my schooling there, Papá? Now you're saying it could be *longer* than two years?"

"We don't know for certain. We have to face the possibility."

"Can't you change your mind?"

I couldn't hold back my sobs as a burst of fear tore through me. I felt vulnerable, unprepared and utterly helpless.

"Please?"

"Our minds are made up," Mamá said, handing me a handkerchief. "Your safety comes first. Besides, Papá and I will join you as soon as the war is over."

"Or I can come home?"

"Yes. Then you can come home."

There was a tense silence.

Flooded with disbelief and dread, I found myself standing on the edge of an abyss.

Do you really know what you're doing to me? I wondered. It's easy for you to say you're sending me to Mexico, but what about me? You're turning my life upside down. What about my friends? I won't have any.

As if she'd read my thoughts, Mamá said, "You'll make new friends in no time, Victor. Knowing you as I do, I'm sure that won't take you long."

I looked at her, and it struck me like a fist in my face. *I have no choice, no say in the matter.*

"How long before I leave, then? If I have to."

"Three weeks," she said. "Whichever ship you're on, I'll come with you on the train, if I can. If not, I'll be at the station to see you off."

"What about you, Papá?"

"I have to return to Bilbao to give these photographs to my friend, George Steer. He's a British reporter for the London *Times*… and the *New York Times*. I was negotiating with him in Guernica after the bombing. The quicker we communicate this atrocity to the world, the better."

"So, if I'm sent on the *Habana* you'll be there?"

"If I'm still in Bilbao. Otherwise, no. I'm sorry."

He stood, walked round the table, took my hand and pulled me to my feet.

He put his hands on my shoulders and looked intently at me.

"I know this comes as a shock. It is a big ask. You might believe you won't cope, Victor, but we know you better than that. You're young. You're adaptable. And even if you have no say in the changes in your life right now, you have control over your attitude towards them. You decide what actions you take. Only you. You understand?"

He gathered me in his arms. "We're depending on you. How you handle every challenge in the future will tell you—and us—the person you are."

When he released me, I sat back stunned, my mind in turmoil.

If I leave, I thought, *my friends will consider me a coward for avoiding the compulsory military call-up most of them will have to do. If I stay, I will consider myself a coward for backing away from the challenges of a future lived alone in Mexico for who knows how long.*

2

As it turned out, the Spanish-American Committee accepted my application a fortnight later to join roughly four hundred and fifty Spanish and Basque children selected to travel to Mexico from Bordeaux.

The day I went to register with Mamá, a lady on the committee handed Mamá a document authorising me to travel through France. She also gave her a white, palm-sized hexagonal cardboard label on which my name and number were printed.

Expedición a Mexico, it read, *Víctor Serrano, No 412.*

She showed me how to wear it on my shirtfront attached with a safety pin.

Then another lady from the committee stepped forward and introduced herself.

"I am Valeria Sánchez," she said, shaking Mamá's hand. "I need your clothes' sizes, Victor. The Mexican Government is going to give you a set of new shirts, trousers, socks and even shoes before you board the ship."

"New clothes?" Mamá asked.

"Exactly. Mexican President Cárdenas had been calling for donations of clothes and money for his 'orphans' as he calls you all. The response across the country has been overwhelming. I've heard you'll even receive a towel and some basic toiletries, with a suitcase to carry them all in. Perhaps also some candies. The voyage has been fully funded, thanks to the generosity of the Mexican people."

Then she asked me if I played chess by any chance.

"Chess? A little," I said, wondering. "I'm learning at school."

Pleased to hear I did, she explained that her ten-year-old son Tomás also played and would be travelling with the group to join relatives in Monterrey.

"He is ten years old and very, very shy." She lowered her voice. "My husband Luis is concerned he may be slightly schizophrenic, or "autistic", if there truly is such a category. He has been researching it. But chess! He plays it all the time and is rarely beaten."

She gazed at me, as though wondering what sort of person I was.

"He's such a perfectionist… but he has difficulties making friends and talking to children his age. I wonder if I could impose on you, Victor, to keep an eye on him. Show him some kindness. Perhaps play a game with him now and then. Otherwise, he'll be left on his own. I know there will be adult *maestras*, teachers and *assistentes* on the ship, but that's not the same. He'll appreciate your attention, but it will take patience and understanding."

"Of course he will," Mamá answered for me, as she often does much to my annoyance. "Won't you?"

"He might help me improve my game," I said.

"Oh, *gracias*, Víctor. Thank you. Luis and I will be in your debt. I'll introduce you to him at the station on Sunday."

3

I knew there was no backing out now. When I was inoculated against smallpox and diphtheria later that week, I was committed.

I soon sorted through the things I was going to take with me. My rock collection to start with. My running spikes. My comics and an assortment of my favourite games, like yoyos and marbles.

Mamá helped me arrange everything into my backpack.

Despite the weight, I was able to carry it on several clumsy practice walks around my bedroom.

I caught the train for Bordeaux in France on Sunday, 23 May.

Papá was at the front somewhere in Asturias, and Mamá couldn't travel on the train with me the day I left. She was an ambulance driver and had to help with the thousands of foreign volunteer fighters pouring in through Valencia and Barcelona to join the International Brigades on the Republican side. She had to arrange transport for them to Madrid, to assist in the relief effort.

She came to the França station though, to see me off.

We met at the station that Sunday morning. About seventy of us. Some as young as three, I remember. Toddlers. One or two older boys looked to be seventeen or more. They were unshaven, sprouting moustaches and the beginnings of beards. They were unaccompanied and looked tough and battle-hardened.

My first thought when I saw them was if they were Basque, at least we had that in common. They made me nervous.

Are they as rebellious as they look? Will they cause trouble on the journey?

I overheard one of the parents say the rest of the groups were already in France. We were the last to leave.'

Wearing our identification labels, we gathered in the cavernous entrance hallway to the station beneath a towering glass dome. A huge bronze ring was suspended beneath it, shining like a giant halo.

I noticed that most of the children were awed into silence when they first arrived, by the crowds, the glare, the gleaming green polished marble and the dome.

But not for long.

They soon broke into a deafening roar in different Spanish dialects, along with some others who were screaming loudly. The noise rose as if someone was turning up the volume in an echo chamber. It seemed to me every child was determined to be heard, especially the young ones who were crying.

When we arrived, Señora Sanchez stepped forward and introduced Tomás.

He was small for ten years old, and thin. And as I'd been warned, extremely shy. He wouldn't look at me at first, except to give me a quick suspicious glance once or twice before turning away. His hair was blond, with a parting straight down the middle. He was wearing round steel-rimmed glasses.

When I tried to shake his hand there didn't seem to be any life in his. He let go of mine at once. He seemed to want to hang onto the cardboard box he was carrying with both hands.

I had never really met anyone like him before. So I smiled to reassure him I meant him no harm. *How am I going to get him to trust me when we're alone?* I wondered.

"As you can see, I have purposefully registered Tomás," Señora Sanchez said. "I've arranged for him to have the number 413. So he'll be standing next to you in every line-up, Víctor. I hope you don't mind."

I nodded briefly. "I agreed to keep an eye on him," I said, wondering what I was letting myself in for. "I'll keep my word.'

At that moment a Spanish *maestra*, a teacher with a loudspeaker, called for calm.

After a lengthy roll call, she led us through to the long curving platform, assisted by four others.

A steam train was drawn up there.

As I walked beneath the station clock, I remember the minute hand jerking down to exactly twenty past eleven.

I had worked out the journey to Bordeaux would take us ten hours. Three to Portbou station, close to the border, where we had to change trains because of the narrower French railway gauge. Another three to Nanterre, where Señora Sanchez told us we'd be staying overnight and changing trains again. Then on to the west coast and our ship.

When we were being shown to our compartment, I asked the assistant if Tomás could come in with me. Which he did.

I could see how upset Señora Sanchez was when he didn't show any emotion at leaving her. He seemed to ignore what was happening around him, as if he wasn't part of what was going on. Until I helped him up to the compartment window as we pulled out. Then he came to life and waved at her.

He never cried.

In fact, throughout the journey to Veracruz in Mexico I never saw him cry.

It was very different for me.

Meeting Tomás and having to relate to him had distracted me from the pain of leaving Mamá. I think she may have felt the same.

I can still remember her last hug, though. She kissed me in the middle of my forehead, like she used to most nights when I was younger and in bed, when she'd tell me without fail before I fell asleep that she loved me. That sent a warm feeling of reassurance surging through me, coupled with deep sorrow that I was leaving her.

She was strong and she was wearing her favourite perfume. I felt her arms tighten around me and smelled her scent on my shirt when I got back on the train. It was like lilacs.

Until I walked into the compartment, where it stank of smoke and soot.

I clearly remember those final confusing moments in the station.

The last-minute shouts and shrilling whistles, the slamming of doors as the train gained traction, steel screeching on steel, steam and smoke erupting across the platform enveloping the crowd blurred through tears I couldn't stop.

Mamá's tall figure in her grey uniform and black hat with distinct white feathers, diminished as the train glided away. It drifted into the left-hand bend, picking up speed, hauling the carriages out into a bleak and overcast day until she was out of sight. The soot-blackened graffiti-covered brick walls beyond the station slid past, the carriages swaying from side to side to the regular clattering rattle of wheels on the tracks.

The clacking echoed in the darkness of my mind as the train gathered speed.

It seemed to be calling out, *There's no going back… there's no going back… there's no going back.*

I closed my eyes and surrendered to the train's vibrations, the distance between everything I was familiar with and the unimaginable future looming ahead widening relentlessly.

It was awful. I had never experienced such dark despair.

I pulled the window halfway down and sat back, waiting for the incoming breeze to clear the sickening smell of smoke and musty upholstery until I became used to it and closed it again.

Then I looked uncertainly at the other three boys in the compartment, before leaning forward and introducing myself.

I was so emotional I didn't pick up their names at once.

It was Tomás who surprised me.

He silently lifted the flap of the table beside the window, then latched it in place. He put the cardboard box he'd been carrying on it, removed the lid and took out a worn folding chess board. Within a minute he had laid out the black and white wooden chess pieces on it, ready for a game.

Then he looked around at each of us in turn, his eyebrows raised and both hands palm up indicating the game.

"Would anyone care to join me?" he asked in a whisper, "I don't like playing on my own."

He sounded so much like a polite and gentle little old man from another century we smiled at one another.

Until he added louder, "Five pesetas a game. Winner takes all," and gave us each an unexpected wink. "Come on, losers. Try me."

His words and gestures were so unexpected and out of character we burst out laughing.

But not for long.

I was his first victim.

Before we reached the outskirts of Barcelona, he'd thrashed me once. By the time we changed trains at Portbou I'd lost another three games and owed him twenty pesetas, which he diligently recorded on a small pad he was carrying in his top pocket.

I was frustrated, but at the same time amused.

When we went through the Balitres tunnel after Portbou, even though the window was now closed and the lights were on, the darkness outside and the deafening clatter of the train distracted Tomás. With his attention elsewhere, I reached out during our sixth game and stole his white knight and queen.

It turned out to be a terrible lesson for me.

When we were back in the sunlight and he saw what I'd done, even though I handed the pieces straight back to him, he tipped them all back into the box along with the board and closed it. Then he clammed up and refused to talk to me or any of the others.

He sat there, clearly hurt and distrustful, as though he'd withdrawn into his own world. He was silent for so long I was worried he'd change compartments or do something desperate, like jump off the train.

I felt awful, like a bully. Which I'm not, but I'd learned something about his inability to understand I wasn't trying to take him down. It was well-meant light-hearted teasing, but he didn't recognise it. He took it personally and responded by switching off. And the other boys laughing at what I'd done didn't help. I had no idea how long it would take him to forgive me, if ever.

We reached Bordeaux late in the afternoon the following day and we reported to the National Evacuation Committee reception centre.

Some Basque and Mexican officials checked us in, and then a short, broad-shouldered Mexican lady in a bright yellow jacket introduced herself as Señora Cortés.

Her thick braided hair was piled up on top of her head and dyed bright red—so bright you couldn't miss her. She stood out like a warning beacon. She told us she was in charge and called out our names through a megaphone, its screech and her deep, no-nonsense voice making my ears pop.

Another Mexican lady handed each of us a blue suitcase. She told us it was packed with clothes and things for the voyage, even candy.

Once we had the suitcase, we had to kneel in front of a young *sacerdote*, a priest—each of us in turn—who blessed us for the journey.

I didn't care so much, but all the older teenage Basque boys refused point blank. Every single one. They were having none of it. They were true Republican socialists—maybe even communists—who had already been fighting on the front lines. They hated the Catholic Church for siding with General Franco's Nationalists.

When I saw their reactions, I knew I'd been right earlier in the station.

There will be fireworks sometime in the future.

It took Tomás two full days to come round, even though we were sharing a room in the Hotel de L'Opéra in Bordeaux.

Señora Cortés had booked us a room there when she ran out of space in the boarding houses where most of the others were staying.

The hotel was a special privilege, and she warned us we had to behave.

It was my first taste of luxury and I've never forgotten it. There were twelve of us booked in, with two Spanish teachers. One of them was Señor Rafael. I liked him. He was easy to talk to and he took an interest in my rock collection.

It wasn't until our second evening at dinner that Tomás spoke to me again. It was the evening before we were due to embark on the *Mexique*.

After the main course, he looked up and asked me, "Did you enjoy the fish?"

They were his first words since the Balitres tunnel incident. I was both relieved and puzzled by the question.

The fish? Did I enjoy the fish?

Before I could answer, he added, "Did you know it was plaice and *not* flounder, as listed on the menu."

I was so surprised I told him no, I didn't.'

"The bony ridge on the head and the orange spots on the skin tell you it's plaice," Tomás assured me. "If you leave the skin on you can see them even after frying. And they've got different scientific names, of course, *Pleuronectes platessa* for plaice and *Platichthys stellatus* for flounder."

I was amazed.

Is he teasing me? I wondered. *A boy of ten talking like an expert on flatfish species. No, he's serious. He's simply stated the facts, unaware of how odd they sounded coming from him.*

"You can check it out on any wall chart with all the European fish listed on it, if you don't believe me," he said, slowly shaking his head and giving me a confidential smile.

Then he stood, folded his napkin, pushed in his chair and picked up the menu.

"What are you doing?" I asked as he walked away. "Where are you going?"

"To the kitchen, to let the chef know," he said. "I'm going to do him or her a favour."

I sat glued to my chair.

Ten minutes later the chef appeared. He was a short, oriental-looking, snub-nosed balding man a little taller than Tomás. He had a crescent of close-cropped silver hair above his ears and around the back of his head. He was wearing a stained, blue-striped apron over his white uniform. He had his chef's hat in his free hand and his arm around Tomás's shoulder as he guided him back to the table.

His brown button eyes twinkled within the folds of the lids as he pulled out the chair and steered Tomás into it.

"*Merci beaucoup, mon jeune monsieur*, thank you, young sir," he said, glancing down at Tomás's name tag. "*Nous vous devons une dette de gratitude*, we owe you a debt of gratitude, Tomás Sánchez. I will talk to the maître de about your correction. When you get the opportunity, please pass on my compliments to your grandfather in his Catalan fish and chip shop you so eloquently described. We will appreciate his recipe if he'll be kind enough to send it to us. I have no doubt it will improve our cuisine."

Then he pushed Tomás's chair in and patted his shoulder.

As he turned to leave, he gave me a wide knowing smile. "Take good care of your friendship," he told me. "You should both value it."

I watched his thick-set body quickstep smoothly as a dancer across the dining room floor to the swing door, where he turned to wave.

"Enjoy your crème brûlée, Tomás," he called out, turning heads at the nearest tables. "The custard is genuine custard and the caramel is caramel. You have my word."

I was astonished.

"Your abuelo owns a Catalan fish and chips shop?" I asked as the kitchen door swung shut. I saw the chef's face peering back through the porthole as he rubbed clear the steam. "Where? In Barcelona?"

"Yes, two. One in El Raval and another in La Rambla," Tomás replied. "They both have big fish charts on the wall. In colour." Elbows on the table, his chin on his hands, he looked at me for a second before his eyes darted away. "That's how I know."

I looked at him across the table, studying him.

I have twelve or thirteen days in the sea air to teach him not to take himself so seriously before I hand him over to his relatives in Veracruz, I realized. *Or at least try.*

The SS Mexique – Courtesy Wikipedia / Creative Commons Attribution

CHAPTER FOUR

1

THE HOTEL DE L'OPÉRA was close to the Richelieu Quay where the *Mexique* was tied up.

When we got to the ship at nine on 27 May, some other groups were already there. There were over two hundred kids milling about. All ages. Many were crying, with several adults trying their best to keep order.

Even though it was a cold and overcast day, the Mexican teachers and their assistants stood out in their bright yellow jackets. They were unmistakable.

Señora Cortés was among them.

When I got closer, I noticed the purple logo embroidered on her pocket. It showed a woman sitting in a chair, nursing an orphan baby on her lap. She had her free arm around another orphan girl standing on her left. The name of the organisation—the *Comité de Ayuda a la Infancia del Pueblo Español*, the Aid Committee for the Children of the Spanish People—was embroidered beneath it.

There were large and rowdy crowds of local people on the quayside who'd gathered to see us off. I thought they must be Spanish and Basque people living in Bordeaux and French workers who may have been Unionists taking time off.

A group among them surprised everyone by singing the Republican songs '*El Ejército del Ebro*' with its rousing '*Ay Carmela!*' chorus, and breaking into '*Viva La Quince Brigada*' now and then. They applauded and threw handfuls of sweets at the children who joined in.

I was astonished by the ship, by the immense size and length of the black hull with red at the waterline. Its central white superstructure rose in two decks to a pair of tall funnels painted dark red with a black band around the top. Barely visible convection currents of exhaust steam were swirling skywards from them. White masts and cranes fore and aft rose above canvas awnings spread across the open promenade decks.

She was magnificent. The biggest passenger ship I'd seen, by far.

But for Tomás it was a different story.

"Fourteen hundred beds," he said, puzzling me as we left the group and walked her length.

"Fourteen hundred beds?" I asked.

"She used to be a hospital ship called the *Lafayette*," he said in a breathless rush. He was so enthusiastic I sensed him stumbling over his words as he struggled to get them out.

"A hospital ship?"

"That's right, a hospital ship. In World War I. Papá told me, and my papá is always right. So there will be plenty of room for all of us. A bed for me and one for you, Víctor. Even food and water, and a bath and toilet, one that flushes back into the sea. We have nothing to worry about. Nothing. If we don't get too close to the rails we'll be safe."

He ran out of wind, took several deep breaths and went on enthusiastically, "We'll be safe, too, because it will never sink. Not like the *Titanic* or *Lusitania*. They only pretended to be unsinkable, but the *Mexique* definitely is. And fast! Seventeen knots at top speed, because she has four propellers. And the latest steam engines drive her, fuelled by oil. Papá is an engineer and he knows. That's why it will only take twelve or thirteen days to get to Veracruz. I'll meet my tía, Matilde Sánchez Salazar there."

"Have you met her before?"

"No."

"Then how will you recognize her?"

"That's easy." He reached for his top pocket and asked, "Would you like to see her?"

"Of course."

He withdrew a clear plastic sachet and showed me a large, round-faced, cheerful-looking woman with a faint moustache. She was wearing a tent-like floral dress imprinted with what I took to be hibiscus flowers. Her black hair streaked with grey hung free in wavy tresses. Her thick arms were crossed beneath pendulous breasts. Her toes protruded through open leather sandals.

I learned more about the ship in those few minutes than I could have read in any brochure.

And I knew I'd have no trouble recognising Tía Matilde when we landed.

2

The ship was due to cast off at three in the afternoon.

We started boarding at ten, after the last group arrived. The tide was on the turn and the River Garonne was rising, its slow-moving water the colour of mud. We climbed the ship's gangway in single file and number order, the angle steepening as the ship rose with the incoming tide.

When it came to my turn, I followed a girl who scrambled up ahead of me. She was shepherding two younger girls in front of her. She looked about thirteen. She was clutching a big black Remington typewriter propped against her left hip with one arm, and her blue suitcase was weighing down her right hand.

She stumbled and almost lost her balance. So I reached up with my free hand to help her.

"Thank you," she said when we reached the deck. "I'm Mercedes Ramos."

I noticed she wasn't wearing a label.

I liked her immediately. Especially the way she blushed, or maybe it was the effort she'd made climbing the gangway. And her eyes were so deep blue they were almost violet.

"We're from Madrid," she told me. "This is my sister Josefina and this little one's Ana. I'm not part of your group. I'm their carer."

"No need for thanks," I said, before I introduced myself, pointing at my label and doing the same for Tomás.

"That's a heavy typewriter," I said.

"Thank goodness it's not a piano," she replied.

I grinned self-consciously. "If it was, I'd come and listen to you play."

I felt my heart thump and wondered if I'd been too forward.

"Oh, that's so romantic, Victor, and we've only just met. You're such a gentleman. I don't play, but if I did at least I'd have an audience of one."

Despite the teasing in her tone, I laughed.

"I might even ask you out afterwards—"

Her eyes lit up with a spark of mockery. I saw the faintest wrinkles at the corners of their lids. "Would you now? And where would you take me?"

Out of my depth now, I stammered, "I'm not sure. I'd have to think about it. To the beach?"

"To the beach? All that sand. How could I refuse?"

Then one of the maestras ordered us to hurry along. I was grateful for the interruption because I sensed Mercedes was teasing me and wasn't sure how to respond.

At the same time, I didn't want her to disappear so soon,

"So, you're a secretary?" I asked, looking back as we separated.

"I'll be working for Señora Cortés. She's getting me to type up the ship's daily newsletter, as well as letters for anyone who prefers that to writing them."

As she turned away, I hoped we'd see more of one another, and wondered if the look she gave me before she went meant she felt the same. I watched her guide her sisters along in front of her until she disappeared through the door to the companionway—but she did not glance back.

Boys and girls were immediately separated, and we were led down port and starboard companionways to the narrow corridors on the decks below. There we were allocated bunks, some four to a cabin, others six and eight.

I was in an outside cabin with a porthole, one deck above the waterline.

Apart from Tomás on the bunk above mine, I soon discovered we had identical twin brothers Fidel and Manuel Echevarria in with us. Long-haired and dark-skinned, they looked like gypsies. And they were so remarkably alike I couldn't tell them apart.

They told me they were Basques from Donostia-San Sebastian. They were my age.

"We're both orphans," Manuel told us, moments after we'd introduced ourselves. "Papá and Mamá are dead. Our papá was a fisherman. One day he went out in his boat and didn't come home."

"Oh. And your mamá?" Tomás asked.

"She died of cancer, or so they thought. Years ago."

"What happened to your papá's fishing boat?"

"He was sailing up the coast to Royan and La Rochelle and back. He was smuggling rifles and ammo back to Spain."

"We don't know if sank in a storm," Fidel broke in, "or maybe hit a mine."

"Or was torpedoed," Manuel said.

"Torpedoed?" I asked, incredulous.

"Possibly," Fidel said. "Hitler had two U-boats working for the Nationalists. They were blockading Bilbao."

"So you're both the sons of a fisherman?"

"Yes, we are," Manuel said.

Without showing it, I smiled inside when things went quiet for a moment.

You two are in for a surprise, I thought. *Tomás is going to test you. It's going to be very interesting to watch. By the time I get to Veracruz, I'll probably have learned the names of every damned fish known. Let alone their colour, shape, bone structure, scaliness and breeding habits. You name it.*

"By the way, how can we tell you apart?" I asked.

"Besides our labels? Easy. I'm Fidel, but I prefer Fid."

"And I'm Manuel, but you can call me Manny."

"How does that help?"

"I've got a mole on my left earlobe," Fid said, lifting a shank of his long hair and revealing it.

"You'll need a haircut so we can see it."

"I've heard the ship's barber is going to give us one. All of us. Soon."

"Even so, anyone who doesn't know about your mole will still be confused. What if you change labels?"

Manny gave a loud burst of laughter. "How do you know we haven't done that already? Just before you came in?"

"I guess we'll have to trust you."

We were confined to the cabin until the ship cast off and we were underway.

We watched the action through the open porthole as the quayside slid away. The hum of engines we'd barely noticed before rose to a deep and regular boom, the vibration of the four propeller shafts bringing the ship to life. The brown water of the Garonne-Gironde River estuary began to swirl beneath us with whirlpools everywhere stirring up the sediment.

We were allowed on deck after sunset.

Tomás and I joined others at the stern, where the red, white and blue French flag billowed in the navigation lights.

The ship was gliding out through the river mouth and the Atlantic lay ahead. I distinctly remember the surface was a fearful black expanse streaked with long diagonal crests of breaking waves. The shimmering wake foamed across the sea behind us towards the coast awash with the lights of villages and the glow of distant Bordeaux.

The giant half-circle of an orange waning moon hung in the haze above the shore. I watched it turn pale and shrink as it rose.

A black and crushing feeling of hopelessness overtook me as it dawned on me it was my last glimpse of Europe for an unpredictable time.

My throat was painfully constricted as I forced myself not to cry. I leaned across the rail and stared at the approaching Atlantic, hoping no one would notice how upset I was.

3

That night the wind strengthened and the rolling movement affected many of us, some worse than others. Many of the younger ones were soon screaming. We heard one or two vomiting in the passageways as they headed for the toilets.

The assistants had their hands full and we had to watch where we trod.

When I began to feel dizzy and then seasick, with my eyes going blurry and my sense of balance distorted, I discovered there were a couple of secret remedies the twins knew.

Manny instructed us to take an apple from the dining saloon that night, which we did.

"Have the apple for breakfast tomorrow," he said. "Just the apple. And stay up on deck in the open air after that, keeping your eyes on the horizon for as long as you can. You'll have your sea legs by the end of the day."

"Our sea legs?" Tomás asked.

"You won't feel seasick anymore."

He also removed Tomás's steel-framed glasses and bent the ends of the temples so that they were tight against the skin behind his ears.

"The pressure will keep you balanced," he explained.

Then he borrowed a matchstick from our *mayordomo de cabina*, our cabin steward. He broke it in half and with great care stuck the pieces behind my ears. He said it would have the same effect. In Tomás's case, it worked like dream. In mine, not so effectively, because I still felt a bit nauseous that night, and when I turned over in bed I was woken by the pain. I removed the matchsticks and was queasy, but never sick.

As for poor Mercedes she reacted badly to the ship's movements the next morning. We met her on the companionway after breakfast, rushing down from the deck above and back to her cabin. She looked terrible. Her skin was light green in the passageway lights.

She had joined the four of us the previous night in the saloon for dinner and she was alright then. In fact, she kept us amused describing her relationship with Señora Cortes, who had taken her on a tour of the ship and shown her where she'd be working in the First Class Library on the upper deck. It was out of bounds to us.

So we had to help her, especially with the younger ones.

Manny tried the matchstick trick with them, but they didn't take kindly to it. It was two full days before they were able to come up out of their cabin. Even then it took Mercedes another day to recover.

The ship's passageways stank of disinfectants for over a week.

That first week was an eye-opener for me.

One thing I discovered was the strange nature of time. It played tricks on me. It stretched out and shortened depending on what I was doing.

For example, when I played chess with Tomás in a corner of the deck or in the saloon as I'd promised, the games were over in minutes. And then time slowed, with the rest of the unplanned day ahead of me. And later in the voyage when Tomás began coaching me, advising me against making dangerous moves and suggesting alternatives, my concentration improved. The games sometimes lasted three and a half hours, but when they ended it often seemed they'd just begun.

It was the same with the short time I was able to spend with Mercedes.

When she was typing during the day or bathing and caring for her sisters in the evening and I had to wait for her, time dragged on; but when we were together for an hour or so on the three delightful times we met, it flashed by until the curfew forced us apart.

I've never forgotten those evenings.

They are imprinted indelibly on my memory.

We spent them leaning across the rail in the bow of the ship, watching the ship's stem below us churning the sea aside in an arrowhead of phosphorescent foam, or sitting side by side on a pair of bollards we found there.

I had never really been alone with a girl I liked before.

At first, I felt shy and awkward. My heart threatened to burst out of my chest and I was tongue-tied.

Fortunately, Tomás was with us that first time and Mercedes put us both at ease.

The Company flag was flying above us on the masthead. It was filling out and falling back as the breeze lifted and fell. Now and then it straightened out, caught the light and cracked like a whip.

"What country's flag does that remind you of?" she asked, pointing up at the red circle on a white background, the word *Transatlantique* printed across the bottom in thick red letters.

"That's easy," Tomás said, beating me to it. "Japan."

"Well done, Tomás," she said. Then she pointed up at the sweep of the Milky Way pulsing with stars that lit up the black sky above our heads. "I'll reach up and give you a gold star for being so quick," she said.

Tomás beamed.

After that it became easier.

By the third and last evening we'd got to know each other well. We'd laughed together so often I felt we'd known one another all our lives.

And the night before we arrived in Veracruz, Mercedes became the first girl I ever kissed. Just the once. I can still feel my arms around her and taste her toothpaste. Like peppermint or cinnamon. And to this day, whenever I taste or smell anything remotely like that combination, I'm back on deck in the dark with her and feeling joyous.

As for the other kids aboard, the older teenagers went wild during the first few days at sea. Especially the Basques, boys and girls both.

Twenty or thirty of them.

It was to be expected.

My instincts had predicted it.

Many had been fighting at the front alongside their parents, defending Bilbao and other places. They'd experienced the war in all its horror. I learned that two had even survived the Guernica bombing.

When the ship left port and we were on the open ocean it seemed the shackles were off. No one was going to tell them what to do or how to behave. They did pretty much as they pleased. Even the younger Basques a year or two older than me were out of control.

Until they discovered there was one line they couldn't cross—the ship's maritime regulations.

Señora Cortés had to call on the chief mate to impose his authority on the third day at sea.

He was a gorilla of a man, with a black unruly beard and thickly muscled forearms. They were covered in so many tattoos you could barely see any skin. He exuded frightening power. His eyes were steely grey. They were colder than my ball-bearing marbles, with no empathy in them at all.

He gathered all the boys who were twelve and over on the front deck, including me, even though I hadn't been involved..

He spoke in French, with one of the Mexican priests translating for him.

He tapped the left shoulder epaulette of his starched white uniform. It carried three gold stripes.

"I am the Chief Mate, and I represent the Captain," he roared in a voice that seemed to reverberate from his barrel of a chest. His expression was ferocious. "I won't hesitate to put any one of you who thinks he can run amuck on my ship in the brig. If you don't believe there is one on a passenger ship, why don't you take me on? I've eaten kids like you for breakfast many times and spat them out."

Then he grinned and showed his teeth. I half-expected to see them filed into sharpened points. "You, you and you," he said, selecting a dozen of the oldest and most rebellious boys, "you all come with me. Now!"

I found out later that he led them down four decks to a cabin in the bowels of the ship with a barred window in its lockable door.

A prison cell.

The news spread like wildfire and the situation quietened down.

The rebels went temporarily into hiding—but not before three of them had bullied Tomás, unfortunately.

On the second day out in the Atlantic, Tomás and I were up on deck before breakfast minding our own business. We were partway through a game of chess,

I had to rush down to the toilet.

When I got back, three older Basques had surrounded poor Tomás and abused him for being "a spoiled rich Catalan kid from Barcelona who hadn't tasted the war yet and needed to be taught a lesson by being thrown to the sharks. It was a lesson they were going to teach him, starting with *this.*"

One of them picked up the white queen, swiping the rest of the pieces across the deck with the back of his hand.

That was the moment I reappeared.

I recognised Julen Gonzáles—he had sat at the table next to us at dinner the night before. I shouted at him in Basque to stop.

He was at the rail, about to fling the piece into the sea.

I sprinted thirty metres to stop him, but I was too late.

I saw the queen sail out across the water as I tackled him.

We ended up wrestling and punching each other in the scuppers for several minutes until two able seamen, who were scrubbing down the decks, rushed over to separate us.

The Basques disappeared into the saloon.

Poor Tomás was stunned. He couldn't speak. I saw the horror on his face before he went down on all fours to gather up the other pieces.

I wiped my bleeding nose and held a handkerchief to it, then told him I'd be back in a moment.'

We were on the second-class deck.

A white rope was slung across the companionway up to first class with an *entrée inderdite* a 'no entry' sign in bold red capitals hanging from it. It was early morning, and I guessed there wouldn't be many first-class passengers up and about, if any.

So I removed my ID label, stepped over the rope and made my way up.

I was right. There were two old gentlemen on a morning walk and a lady in a deckchair with her feet up on the rail, reading. They took no notice of me.

In the saloon library, I found what I was looking for—a bookshelf dedicated to board and card games like backgammon, drafts, chess, packs of cards, even a French version of Monopoly. I opened a box of plastic chess pieces, rummaged among them for the white queen and pocketed it before strolling nonchalantly back to Tomás.

"How did you know there was a chess set up there?" Tomás asked, wide-eyed, when I handed him the replacement. "Have you been up there before?"

"Mercedes described the library to us at dinner the other night. Remember?" I said. "She was shown up there the day we boarded because she's Señora Cortés's secretary and will be working there."

"I can't keep that," he said.

"Why not?"

"Because you stole it."

"Some rules were meant to be broken, Tomás. Considering what you've been through today you deserve to have this piece in exchange. To complete your set."

"What about anyone who wants to play chess in First Class?"

"There are several sets up there. They'll be fine. Besides, it will be something for you to remember me by."

When we set the pieces up, the plastic white queen didn't match the other wooden pieces, and she was so much taller than the rest she looked comically out of place.

Tomás saw the funny side and smiled like the sun had broken through.

That morning was one of the few times I saw him smile that way.

I knew I was winning him over.

5

VICTOR: In Havana, Cuba, June 3, 1937

We were on deck with a crowd of other children a week later, on Thursday afternoon 3 June, peering down at the timber pilot boat manoeuvring alongside the *Mexique*. It was blowing a gale and she was pitching sickeningly in a turbulent sea a kilometre offshore from Havana in Cuba.

The lighthouse and grey walls of Morro Castle stood out on a rocky promontory at the mouth of the entrance canal to the port.

We watched the Cuban pilot stretch his right leg across the gap to the rope ladder slung down the ship's side as it swung out towards him. He promptly climbed several wooden rungs with surprising agility before hanging on as the pilot boat bore away. Then the ladder hurled him back against the hull as if it was determined to dislodge him.

He had his briefcase slung across a shoulder

After several violent rolls of the ship and repeat performances, he clambered through the gate in the railing and onto the deck.

When we cheered and applauded him, he swept off his cap as and gave us a bow, as though there was nothing to it.

I've never forgotten him.

I can see him climbing like he's doing it right here, right now. Like a monkey in a smart blue suit. He made it to the top and never lost his nerve, or his cap. He reminded me of Papá's advice—set yourself a purpose in life and take it one rung at a time, like he did. Then keep climbing, no matter how difficult it gets or impossible it seems, no matter what life throws at you.

Two hours later the ship was moored alongside the Sierra Maestra quayside in the flat calm, protected from the storm brewing far out to sea.

It was our first port of call and welcome relief from the empty ocean.

We were there for only one day and weren't allowed ashore, but the plaza in front of us was full of people. They were as keen to see us as the crowds had been in Bordeaux. Our story had preceded us.

We'd become famous across the world.

As for the old-fashioned cars driving past now and then, I'd never seen anything like it—a stream of vintage Lincolns, Pontiacs, Chevrolets and Fords covered in chrome. Many had white-walled tyres. Their scarlet, primrose yellow, emerald green and sapphire blue enamelwork was polished to a sheen. Their horns blared as they paraded past, as pristine as they'd been the day they'd come off the assembly line.

We loved it.

And Fid was car mad.

He outdid Tomás for once, as they competed in listing the makes and models and noting their number plates as they passed. Some of them must have been driving a circular route though, because Fid recorded their makes and number plates again and again, so often that Manny and Tomás accused him of cheating.'

We were asleep when the *Mexique* put to sea again, but were abruptly woken in the early hours when the wind rose and the weather worsened. It became so bad we had to raise the safety boards to prevent ourselves from rolling out of bed.

It became wilder and wilder.

The ship rolled one way and shuddered before surging back the other in what Manny described as a "corkscrewing" motion. We saw the ship's work lights through the porthole as they reflected on foaming water sweeping up the dark side of the hull one moment, before rushing back towards the roaring crests of breaking waves the next. They were driven by a yowling wind.

Just at dawn the heavens opened and the rain thundered down. Then we couldn't see anything. The water rushing down the glass flashed now and then with blinding lightning strikes.

Fid and Manny were in their element.

"It's just like coming home to San Sebastián in the winter! With the tanks full of mackerel and herring and a thunderstorm working us over in the Bay of Biscay," Fid said.

Then Manny replied, "That's the storm showing its teeth. Let's go up on deck and see what it's like."

Moments later, Manny opened the cabin door. He peered into the corridor and beckoned us out. We followed him towards the aft companionway, meeting no one. We held both arms outstretched to ward off the bulkheads as the ship's long, shuddering pitching hurled us from side to side.

We climbed two levels and moments later Manny leaned his shoulder into the port side door to the deck. It opened a crack, but the wind was too strong and slammed it shut. The starboard door swung open when he tried it though, and we watched him stagger across the slippery teak deck. He was like a drunkard fighting for balance. His angled body stepped crazily uphill on the spot one moment, before being propelled down to the rail the next.

His triumphant shriek of laughter was torn away by the crosswind as he slammed into the rail. He leaned out over the raging water, the gale whipping at his hair.

Tomás followed him out.

I tried to hold him back, but he slipped under my arm.

When he was halfway across, he lost his footing.

The wind picked him up and tossed him sideways, like a discarded puppet.

He slid diagonally on his backside into the scuppers, laughing, so his mouth was open when the second rail struck his face, splitting his lip and breaking off a segment of his right-hand front tooth.

When he turned to face us, still laughing, he looked like someone with a cleft lip. He spat a mouthful of blood into his hand and caught the triangular piece of enamel in his fist.

Then he said something I've never forgotten.

He looked up at Manny, showed him the fragment and yelled, "*That's* the storm showing its teeth."

It was the first time I'd heard him poke fun at himself on the spur of the moment. It cracked us up. How he didn't lose his glasses I'll never know, unless it was because Manny had tightened the temples.

When the three of us dragged him back through the door, his reaction amazed me.

Never mind the split lip and the blood, the fragment of broken tooth in his hand was like a holy relic. A touchstone. He didn't complain about the pain or the swollen disfigurement or the ship's doctor giving him five stitches to seal the wound.

In fact, after we'd cleaned him up and he saw the gap in his front teeth in the cabin mirror, he seemed overjoyed. Even when he heard the comical lisp it caused with certain sounds.

I believe he felt he'd passed some sort of test.

He'd lived dangerously.

Taken a chance.

He'd proved himself to us, but more so to his previous self.

He'd come of age at ten years old, in some strange way known only to himself.

Just as well Señora Sánchez isn't on board, the thoughts raced through my mind. *She'd eat Manny alive, let alone me. On the other hand, has Manny done him an unexpected favour? Given him an opportunity to do what boys do? Take a risk, even though he came off second best? No risk, no gain. It's given him something to brag about to others with confidence and pride. Something he has never done before. He has learned to treat misfortune with humour and irony.*

Especially considering what he did next.

6

VICTOR: In Veracruz, Mexico, June 7, 1937

Four days later, we approached Veracruz on the Mexican coast just after dawn.

The breeze was gentle when Tomás and I were at the rail watching the hazy coastline take clearer shape. The lighthouse beam swept across the copper-coloured sea, flecking the waves with light as it passed across them.

Flocks of screaming gulls swooped and wrestled in wild and bickering zigzags to catch the crusts of bolillo buns a few of the younger children had scavenged from the dining room and were throwing at them.

"Seventeen knots at top speed," Tomás suddenly reminded me. "It's taken us exactly twelve days to get here. Papá was right."

He looked me in the eye for longer than usual, which I found both pleasing and disconcerting, before he explained something I didn't expect.

His papá was right? Here we go again, I thought. *What will it be like this time?*

"Seventeen knots. That's *nothing*, Victor. You want to know something else?"

Before I had a chance to answer, he reeled off a breathless series of facts as though he was reading from an encyclopaedia.

"The earth is forty thousand kilometres round at the equator. Roughly. It spins once every twenty-four hours. So we're travelling at four hundred and sixty metres a second if you live on the equator, in Ecuador, say. *A second.* That's around one thousand, six hundred and seventy kilometres an hour." He took a deep breath, before telling me we were, "Also going around the sun once a year *even faster*. At thirty *kilometres* a second. That's one hundred and eight thousand kilometres an hour."

When he'd finished, he smiled at me as though he'd passed some sort of oral examination and deserved a pat on the back.

I was so astonished I stood there shaking my head.

It was the first time I'd heard him express himself with such enthusiasm since describing the *Mexique* as an ex-hospital ship or discovering the error with the flatfish. As for his calculations, I had no idea how accurate they were, but if his papá had told him, well.

"If we're spinning that fast, how come we don't fly off?" I asked, smiling to humour him and see what he'd say.

"Easy. Gravity. It holds us down. Yes, we're spinning, and centrifugal force is pushing us outwards. But gravity is stronger." Then he grinned. "If it wasn't we'd be flung out into space."

"Did your papá tell you that?"

"No... yes, in a way. I read it and then I asked him if it was true."

We soon discovered that if we'd been famous in Bordeaux and Havana, it was nothing compared to what greeted us in Veracruz.

There must have been thousands packed along the dock and on the promenade under the palm trees beyond the warehouses. They were all decorated with flags and balloons.

The city had been given the day off work, I found out later.

A long white banner was slung between palm trunks. It read, "*El pueblo Mexicanos da la bienvenida a los huérfanos de España*", "The Mexican People Welcome the Spanish Orphans".

Several officials were seated on a central dais facing us as we pulled alongside.

A row of privileged men and women in front of them cooled themselves with fans and flattened programs. They were facing away from the ship, but craning their necks to look back up at us.

Behind them, lines of empty benches stretched along the quay. We would use them when we disembarked.

To the left was a loud military brass band with twenty or so red-capped musicians with gleaming instruments. They were dressed in starched white uniforms. Red stripes ran down the sides of their trouser legs and their shoulder epaulettes were encrusted with gold braid. They were pumping out patriotic tunes as the gangway was lowered. I recognized a few that were Spanish, but the rhythms they used were somehow different from ours and didn't seem right.

It was hot.

They looked as if they were melting with sweat.

Two Red Cross ambulances were parked to the right. A group of first aid nurses squatted on the quay in the shade beside them.

Señora Cortés and her team of maestras and assistants had a hard time gathering the over-excited younger children together, checking their belongings and then lining us all up along the decks in number order.

Just before we headed for the gangway, Tomás tugged my shirt and pulled me aside.

He handed me his chess set.

"This is for you," he said, "because you are my friend and you can practice all the moves I've taught you on it."

I was speechless.

How can I accept it? It's so important to him.

"And so is this," he went on before I could reply.

He reached into his back pocket and pulled out a menu from the first-class dining saloon.

"I have marked it so you won't forget me."

On the back was a picture of the *Mexique* in full colour. On the front was the menu for last night's dinner—Sunday, 6 June. He'd written the words "*SOLEA SOLEA*" beside the main course of "*Grilled Dover Sole Niçoise*".

"I've written out the fish's scientific name for you. In capitals. Easier to read."

When I asked him where he'd found the menu, he replied that he'd taken off his ID and stepped over the rope across the first-class companionway late yesterday afternoon.

"Like you did when you went up and stole the white queen for me."

He'd walked into the dining room like any other first-class passenger, picked up a menu from the batch beside the door and walked out with it as if he belonged there and was entitled to it.

He laughed aloud when he saw me shake my head.

"Some rules are meant to be broken," he said. "You taught me that, and you're my best friend so you can't be wrong. It will be something for you to remember me by."

"But I have nothing to give you, Tomás."

He lifted his upper lip and tapped his triangular front tooth.

"You have already. This. The plastic queen," he said, "and some other things I won't forget."

It has taken a broken tooth for him to come out of his shell, I thought.

Morelia Catholic Cathedral / Courtesy Roberto Galan / Alamy stock photos

CHAPTER FIVE

1

WHEN WE AND THE adults guiding us were eventually seated on the benches, the master of ceremonies stepped up to the microphone and introduced the Minister of Foreign Relations, Ernesto Hidalgo, who was seated to his right.

He was a tall man with a receding hairline, smartly dressed in a khaki safari suit. The hot sun gleamed from the sweat on his balding head as he stepped up to the microphone.

His speech was very brief. I got the feeling he couldn't wait to sit back down.

"I am here to welcome you poor children to Mexico," he said, then turned and pointed at another official seated behind him, "and hand you over to our Minister for Education, Luis Orozco. Now that you have all arrived safely in Mexico, my job is done."

His sing-song southern Mexican-Spanish accent was difficult to follow. We looked at each other, trying not to smile, but giggling broke out and got worse because the seated teachers and assistants could only glare at us and hiss.

Then the second Minister came to the microphone.

Short, plump and red-faced, with a black beard streaked with grey and a mass of white hair swept straight back, he was the opposite of the previous speaker.

His voice was deep and resonant. He caught my attention.

"*Ustedes cachorillos del viejo león español,*" he began, "you cubs of the old Spanish lion, I am pleased to tell you *las alas del águila ázteca*, the wings of the Aztec eagle are now ready to protect you."

I could see that most of us had no idea what he meant.

Then he read us a copy of a message telegraphed that morning from President Cárdenas to the Republican Spanish President.

"I can assure you your orphans will be treated with great affection. They will receive an education fit for the second generation of children after the Mexican revolution. They will become the future defenders of their new country, according to the constitution of 1917."

Future defenders of our new country? I wondered. *And we're somehow mentioned in the Mexican Constitution? I'm totally confused.*

For the first time it struck me that we may not be refugees temporarily transferred to safety in Mexico, who would repatriate in a year or two. We might find ourselves instead caught in a political net, from which we may never escape.

Especially when he confirmed that since we were all orphans, we would immediately be declared wards of the Mexican state.

I was shocked and horrified.

I'm not an orphan or a ward of the Mexican State! I'm Basque first, Spanish second and a citizen of the world third. Papá has always taught me that. Now I'm about to become a Mexican? No way!'

When the speaker said that, a large woman standing to one side in the crowd interrupted him.

She tore off her wide-brimmed straw hat and shouted, "*Todos no son huérfanos!* They are *not* all orphans!"

She wagged her forefinger and pointed at Tomás, who was sitting next to me.

"That is my nephew, Tomás Sánchez, and his mother and father are alive and well. They live in Barcelona. I have come to take him back to Monterrey."

The drama was riveting.

Then I recognised her. It was his Tía Matilde in the photograph.

Two municipal policemen rushed up, grabbed her by the elbows and wrestled her away. She couldn't shake them off. As they dragged her towards the warehouses she looked back and screamed that she'd give them his parents' Barcelona address so they could check. They forced her to the back of the crowd. I saw a gaunt man bent over his walking stick limping after them. I assumed he was her husband.

Later, I found out I was right when he and Señora Matilde came over to take Tomás away.

Poor Tomás.

He surprised me by hugging me and hanging on, as though I was his *manta de seguridad*, his security blanket. He was so desperate they had to drag him off.

It was very moving.

I'll never forget it.

There I was, his chess set under my arm and his menu in my suitcase, and I realised it was the first time I'd seen him crying. It was as if he didn't know how to stop. He was still sobbing when they shut him in the back of their car and drove away.'

As for Mercedes, she'd already gone ashore much earlier.

I saw her on the dockside wearing a yellow jacket like the

one Señora Cortés wore. She was with one of the Mexican damas on the committee, who was holding Ana's hand and leading the three of them to a bus. Josefina was the first to climb aboard. Mercedes next.

She turned and waved at the ship from the top step and I waved back, but I don't think she saw me because everyone along the rail was waving.

That was the last time I ever saw her.

Later that month, when I found out her address in Puebla, I sent her a letter from Morelia. Then I received a postcard she sent from the convent where she was a receptionist and carer for young girls.

'There is no point, Victor,' she wrote. 'Don't be sad. Remember what we talked about last night on board the ship? I told you shipboard romances never last, and you said why don't we try? Well, I was right. We're living too far apart…'

There's no point? Don't be sad?

I didn't read on, and I didn't reply.

I tore it up.

2

I found myself in a compartment with several of the older and wilder Basque boys on the train to Mexico City late that evening.

I was the youngest in the group, and I was silent for most of the journey.

The sun soon set, and the train rattled on through the darkened countryside.

Behind us the older Basques were smoking and flinging crude observations and obscenities across the compartment. I listened to the disgruntled and mutinous comments as I played two-handed Chinchón into the night with one Basque boy who had befriended me, Félix Arostegui, two years older than me.

We lifted our cards with a flourish while we still had the energy, slapping them down hard on the tabletop between us as we formed sets of matching suits.

I had my back to them, but couldn't help overhearing their conversation. It was a new experience for me, and I couldn't stifle my laughter every now and then.

"*Malditos huérfanos!* Fucking orphans! I'll give them fucking orphans. I'll rip the feathers off their Aztec eagle's wings." I recognised Luka Garcia's voice.

"What do they take us for? They think we're made of putty they can shove around? The wankers can think again," Julen Gonzáles said. He was the Basque boy I'd fought the day he flung Tomás's queen overboard. We had since declared a truce.

"If they think at all." Luka agreed. "And lion *cubs?* Bloody hell, *lions* more like it. The things I've seen. The things I've had to do! *He probado mi coraje*, I've already tested my courage, and now I'm going back to school to learn how to become a bloody Mexican patriot? And they're going to throw away the key? No chance in hell."

"And those damn maize tortillas they served up," I heard Luis Velasco's shrill voice interrupt. "*Maize.* Filled with beans and rice. You ever tasted chillies like it? Jesús, they were hot. I'll be shitting flames for weeks, not to mention my exploding farts."

I looked at Felix who was holding his next card high in the air and we both burst out laughing.

"If you need first aid for that," Julen said, "those nurses were *agradable a la vista*, easy on the eye. Did you see them sitting beside the ambulances? Chicks ripe for plucking."

"Maybe that's why they were there, to put our fiery arseholes out with the Lulú apple soda they served up. One good shake of the bottle and point." Mikel Fernández spoke for the first time.

"And these bags of Larín candy they've given us. Sickly sweet. Maybe we can use them to sweet talk Rosita Diego or Sabina Marcos to put out for us again," Julen suggested. "At least it won't be in the damn lifeboat next time."

"Hey, talking of sweets and lifeboats," Luka said, "we must have finished the condensed milk in the survival rations in all the boats within a week of leaving Bordeaux."

"Larín candy—now there's a thought. I've still got a bag. Here, you want one? There are a few sweet and sours left." Mikel said.

"Save a sweet one for Rosita." I heard a voice I didn't recognise.

"I prefer sour Sabina, even if she is a bitch. More meat, and always ready for butchering as they say," Luis said.

"I'll keep her in mind, wherever we end up," the voice I hadn't recognised spoke up.

Wherever we end up? I wondered, half asleep. *In Morelia, of course. Sent there by Mamá and Papá for my own good. Getting an education at the Spanish-Mexican School.* Then my thoughts became confused and I realised how tired I was. *Putting my best foot forward and becoming who I am… by discovering the self I'm growing into… when I always thought I was who I am already…*

I put down my last card, yawned and stretched out on the bench, no longer able to resist the rocking of the carriage.

3

VICTOR: In Mexico City and Morelia, Mexico, June 8, 1937
The number of people who came out on the streets to greet us in central Mexico City blew my mind.

President Cárdenas had declared a holiday for public servants and schoolchildren, getting maximum exposure for his generosity. He left nothing to chance. We could hardly move at the station when we arrived.'

Watching the flashbulbs go off at the station made me uneasy.

Anxious, to the pit of my stomach.

Even the international press was there, I discovered, when our pictures appeared in newspapers delivered to the school later that month. The teachers got us to cut them out and pin them to the noticeboards.

Yes, the president was doing us a great favour in granting us asylum, but he was taking credit for it around the world.

I was missing Papá and Mamá terribly.

I was beginning to realise how alone I was, facing the frightening ordeals that lay ahead on my own. I had to find the courage to dig deep. Dig a trench if I had to, so that I could duck for cover when the bullets started flying.

I was now sure they would.'

I'd seen how cruel the Basque boys could be and wondered how long it would be before life in Morelia brought out the worst in them.

We arrived in Morelia two days later, and were driven to the *Escuela España-México*, the Spanish-Mexican Industrial School in a fleet of buses.

It was a converted convent. Two large buildings stood on grounds enclosed behind a two-metre-high wall of red brick. Every ten metres there were metre-wide architectural gaps lined with vertical steel palings, their points sharp as spears.

The bus driver told us an electrified wire ran across the top right around the perimeter.

"You'll all be safe in there," he said over the speaker. "No one will get in."

"Or out," I heard Mikel Fernádez mutter under his breath.

Heavy wooden double gates sealed the main entrance. I read the name of the school carved into the granite archway as the bus drove under it,

It was both welcoming and foreboding—I was relieved we'd finally arrived, but unsure what was in store. Especially when I saw two workmen scrubbing graffiti from the front wall and read the words painted there in whitewashed capitals:

AL DIABLO CON LOS HUÉRFANOS ESPAÑOLES—
CUIDA A NUESTROS HUÉRFANOS MEXICANOS
PRIMERO
TO HELL WITH THE SPANISH ORPHANS—TAKE
CARE OF OUR MEXICAN ORPHANS FIRST

That really shocked me.

We weren't as popular as we believed.

I wondered how long our welcome would last, especially after what happened one hot weekend in early August, when we'd been there for six weeks.

The principal had allowed us to spend Sunday in the city.

Manny, Fid and I were sitting on the grass in the Plaza de Armas in the city centre having lunch. We could hear what sounded like a riot a street away, getting closer.

Then a rowdy mob of older kids, most of them Basques I recognised, burst past us.

Félix was among them. When he saw us he stopped, jogged across to a nearby flowerbed and removed a handful of rocks from the border. He dropped them at our feet.

"*Si no estás con nosotros, estás contra nosotros*, if you aren't with us, you're against us. Follow me!"

Then he tore after the others who were breaking into the Catholic cathedral.

Once they got inside, an ear-shattering uproar broke out. We watched in shock as stained-glass windows were smashed, rocks thrown from the inside exploding out and scattering multicoloured shards across the paving.

Mingled with the confused screams and shouting, we heard the crash of furniture being overturned and metal ornaments flung against the walls.

Then we smelled smoke, a black cloud rising through a smashed window.

We were horrified.

At first, we joined the crowd of Morelianos who were rushing to the plaza to watch, and then took the wisest course—we hurried back to school. We could hear the sirens of the fire brigades behind us as we ran and saw a bus filled with armed National Guardsmen flying down Francisco I Avenue towards the cathedral.

That incident was a turning point.

President Cárdenas himself visited the school with a team of advisers the following day. Michoacán was his home state, Morelia the capital. I found out later he lived in a house overlooking Lake Cuitzeo, north of the city.

He was an extraordinary man.

Over five days he met every single child, from the youngest to the oldest.

When I met him on the second day, he assured me it was his humanitarian duty to take care of me, and take care of me he would, provided I reciprocated with good behaviour, showed respect for the Mexican flag, and was willing to learn according to Mexico's socialist curriculum.

"How do you feel about that?" he asked.

Tongue-tied, I stammered that I would.

"So what do you want to become? What profession?"

"A geologist or a geophysicist."

He raised his eyebrows, pursed his lips and slowly nodded,

He got one of his assistants to note that on my record.

"I will be watching your progress with special interest from now on, Victor. You'll be happy to hear I'm planning to establish an *instituto politécnico nacional*, a technical university in Mexico City for engineering students next year. If you apply yourself to your studies, who knows? There may be a place there for you when you graduate."

When the president left, thirty-two of the ringleaders, including Félix, were transferred back to Veracruz and enrolled in an industrial school attached to a prison for young offenders there. The following month two groups of older girls who'd been wandering the streets were moved to convents in Guadalajara and Mexico City.

By December 1937, our numbers had been reduced by sixty-five. These included those expelled to Veracruz or sent to convents, six who'd run away and hadn't been caught, three young ones who had died, and several children under three years of age who had been adopted out.

The atmosphere was calmer after that, especially when Señor Rafael López replaced the previous school principal.

He was an imposing Nahua part-Indian mestizo— stocky and broad-shouldered.

He was a strict authoritarian with a full head of jet-black hair he had a habit of running both hands through. His thick black eyebrows protruded above glittering green eyes set wide apart. He wore a classic moustache concealing his upper lip.

"I am here because I know how to turn failing schools around," he told us grimly the day he arrived. "President Cárdenas has appointed me to do exactly that. Take that as a warning."

He carried a bamboo cane everywhere he went. He called it "el zap", his "*zapatista*"—named after the left-wing campesino peasants he told us he'd fought beside during the uprising in 1918.

When he gathered the senior boys together on his memorable first day, he introduced us to "el zap". He lifted it over his head and whipped it viciously through the air with a fearsome whizzing sound. He repeated the action in case anyone hadn't heard it the first time, then struck a desktop with a deafening *thwack*!

"I won't hesitate to use it," he assured us. "I will cane anyone who steps out of line. Without hesitation. Who'd like to be the first? I will put the boot in."

We called him "*el zapato*" behind his back after that—the bootmaker.

It didn't take him long to demonstrate he meant business and we knew we'd met our match,

Señor López's message was clear, and the school was different from the day he arrived.

I thought he was a breath of fresh air.

He got rid of several teachers and appointed others more to his liking.

They were left-wing socialists, even communists, it seemed to me. He believed our relationship with them would be less tense than it had been with the Catholics among those he sacked. He was right, especially among the older Basque and Catalan boys still with us who hated the Nationalist Catholic Church.

Then, after several weeks of observing everyone, he selected a group of eight senior boys and girls he appointed as *prefectos escolares*. School prefects. To organise and discipline the children allocated to their teams.

From then on everything changed.

By the beginning of February 1938, our lives were strictly disciplined and followed a regular routine, like a military school.

We had our daily chores, including keeping the grounds and gardens in good order, an early morning run and cold showers. Classes till midday, then a rest and afternoon study till four. After that, sport was compulsory.

Soccer was not for me, but basketball, yes. And sprinting. I was quick over two hundred metres and I'd brought my spikes. Not the fastest, but fast enough. I won once or twice over the years, but was second or third most of the time.

"You were beaten by a nose again, Pinocchio," Fid told me once. "Yours isn't long enough yet. Perhaps you're too honest!"

Senor López also appointed two buglers, two Mexican boys who could play, to blow their instruments at certain times and measure out the days.

I became lifelong friends with one of them—Guillermo Reyes. He was a Tepehuán Indian mestizo from Durango.

Guillermo shared my interest in rocks and helped me with my guitar playing.

The bugle calls woke us first thing in the morning at six, then at eight-thirty after breakfast for assembly and a flag-raising and pledge-taking ceremony. And then again in the evening at six, when the flag was taken down before dinner.

Whenever the bugle sounded, we had to stand to attention wherever we were and face the flagpole. Even when we were indoors.

One morning two years later, Director López, called me from my class and showed me into his office. A stranger was in there and the principal left us together.

I thought at first, he was Vladimir Lenin, the likeness was so striking. I knew that Lenin was a leader in the Russian Revolution in 1917. We had a picture of him among other socialist political leaders on a classroom wall.

The stranger had the same lean and bony face, the high round forehead and sweep of eyebrows over hypnotic Asian eyes. Their piercing gaze was frowning at the light, or maybe it was short-sightedness. He had the same straight nose and beard around his unsmiling mouth.

He removed a pair of rimless glasses from the top pocket of his black suit, polished the lenses on a scarlet handkerchief and placed them on his nose. He peered at me over them, then pushed them up the bridge of his nose with his middle finger and examined me through them.

"Víctor," he said, "you won't remember me. I met you once when you were only four. Now you've grown up, but you're exactly as Xavier described you. I could have picked you out in a crowd. I am pleased to meet you. I am Kurt Lessing, a friend of your father."

His Spanish was poor, his accent broken. *He must be German*, I thought, *or Scandinavian.*

"I've brought you some things Xavier wanted you to have." He shook my hand and then patted the seat of a chair he'd arranged facing his. "Sit. Make yourself comfortable. Don't be nervous."

A worn but polished brown leather briefcase was propped against the leg of his chair.

He picked it up, placed it on his lap and fiddled with the buckle. He didn't open it but sat there patting it and shaking his head without looking at me for almost a minute. He mumbled something to himself I couldn't understand. I think he was talking in Yiddish or some German dialect. It sounded as if he was praying. Perhaps he was.

He turned to me. "I tell you not to be nervous when I should be telling myself. You must prepare yourself, my boy. I bring you sad news."

He leaned forward and placed a hand on my shoulder. "Perhaps we get that out of the way first."

He handed me his scarlet handkerchief, and without further hesitation, told me my papá Xavier was no longer of this world.

"He faced a firing squad against the wall of La Modelo prison in Barcelona. He died six months ago, on 29 January," he said.

What he'd just announced seemed to deafen me.

I watched in horror as he kept talking, mouthing words I no longer heard or understood.

It was horrifying, as if a door had slammed shut in my face.

I screamed at him to stop.

The space between us turned black and the room spun as if I'd fallen from a precipice. How long it lasted I have no idea.

I clung to my chair until my vision gradually cleared and his blurred face reappeared. We stared at one another for a full minute. It's as close to madness as I've ever come.

Kurt placed the briefcase on the floor and stood behind me, squeezing my shoulders with both hands, before pouring a glass of water for me from a jug on a sideboard to his left. "Be brave," he said, as he handed it to me and sat down again. "This is hard for you, I know."

I could see him thinking it was as hard for him to tell me about it as it was for me to hear it.

He went on to describe how Xavier had been arrested on 26 January, while photographing refugees retreating through the streets of Barcelona.

"It was a so-called citizen's arrest," he explained. "We were together at the time, when a gang of fifth columnists sympathetic to Franco seized him outside the Vallcarca hospital. They must have been hiding in the neighbourhood. They held me as well, until they saw my German papers. They handed Xavier over to a detachment of Nationalist *regulares* soldiers who were looting nearby shops and houses at the time, street by street."

Kurt lifted the briefcase to his lap again and withdrew a photograph album. I recognised it as Abu Xavier's at once. He flicked through several pages before handing it to me open at a page with several photographs.

"Take a look at these photos," he said, pointing. "There was a film in Xavier's camera and these shots were on it. They were the last ones he ever took. Before his arrest, he handed his camera to me for safekeeping while he went to assist one of the wounded patients from the hospital."

He leaned across and pointed with a forefinger.

"That old man there, the one with both legs missing. He must have crawled down the steps and Xavier was helping him sit more comfortably against the wall. He was about to arrange the blanket over him when he was arrested."

The photos showed several corpse-like starving figures, mutilated and bandaged, wearing ragged striped pajamas. They were staggering down the hospital steps. One of them was limping towards the line of refugees passing in the street. His mouth was a gaping black hole as though he was pleading not to be left behind.

The nearest refugees escaping the city were hauling and pushing two overloaded carts up the slope. One was hauled by a skinny mule, the other with two old men straining against the shaft. Two women and a young girl were stooping to place rocks behind the rear wheels to prevent the carts from rolling backwards as they made their way uphill.

The old double amputee, breath steaming, sat half-naked in the freezing cold against the wall, watching. The rumpled blanket lay beside him as if he hadn't the strength to spread it over himself.

"You can see why Xavier went to help the old man," Kurt said.

He told me they took Xavier to the La Modelo prison. He was held there for three days. He gave Kurt the keys to his house, and Kurt was allowed to take food and the latest local newspapers to him.

When Kurt visited the prison on the last day, the guards told him Xavier had been executed the night before by firing squad. They lined him up with several others and shot him for his sympathies with the Republican cause and for the work of his wife, Marina Serrano, with the International Brigades.

"They told me Xavier's body had been delivered to the mass grave at the Fossar de la Pedrera, the Cemetery of the Quarry on Montjuïc," he said.

When he'd finished, Kurt emptied the briefcase.

He handed me Abu's Leica camera and a batch of photographs, newspapers and magazines.

He told me he'd arranged with Director López for me to take three days of leave from school. He and his wife Frida were staying at the Hotel de la Soledad before continuing to Los Angeles.

"You are very welcome to stay with us if you wish."

6

They were stressful days.

I don't know how I'd have survived if I hadn't gone with him.

I was overcome with grief, especially when I met Señora Lessing.

I will never forget her. She was a short, rather plump and motherly woman with blond hair and a pale round face. She was wearing a midnight blue dress, darker than her light blue eyes. I saw them filled with concern when we met.

Although she spoke no Spanish, her sympathetic voice was warm and comforting. The moment she gently hugged me for the first time in the courtyard of the hotel, murmuring her condolences beside my ear, I broke down and couldn't stop crying.

It's strange.

I can still feel the softness of her body and the warmth of her breath, as well as smell her perfume when I recall that afternoon. A fresh and delicate scent like Mamá's lilacs.

For the next two days, waves of grief washed through me when I least expected them. They even woke me in my sleep, but by the third day I felt I was getting stronger.

I willed myself to be.

Kurt told me one evening after dinner as the waiter was clearing away the empty plates, that he was a camera technician. "I am an expert with lenses," he said. "That's how I met Xavier. I worked for Leica, for Ernst Leitz and his daughter Elsie, in Wetzlar. During the civil war, I used to accompany Xavier and other photographers in the war zones for months at a time, checking how the cameras performed in action, looking for improvements."

He was Jewish, he went on, and the Nazis were targeting Jews during the 1930s. After *Kristallnacht* in November 1938, Ernst Leitz began arranging travel permits to save the lives of hundreds of his Jewish employees to get them out of Germany.

"Frida and I were among the last to escape. We left France aboard the SS *Sinaia*, from the port of Sète," he said. "We arrived in Veracruz a fortnight ago, along with the first sixteen hundred exiled Republicans looking for asylum."

He pushed back his chair and stood. "Stay here," he said. "I'll be back in a minute. I have some papers a group of us refugees printed during the voyage in my room. I think they'll interest you. They might remind you of your trip aboard the *Mexique*."

He returned a moment later and handed me a sheaf of twelve folded news sheets.

"These will give you something to read while you're here."

That night I read the banner of the first edition. It was dated 25 May, 1939, the day the ship left France: *SS Sinaia— the Diary of the First Expedition of Spanish Republicans to Mexico.*

When I'd read the cover and turned the page, a surprising illustration on page two caught my eye.

A hand-drawn aircraft, stalled and falling through the clouds, was spiralling down towards the desert sands of the Sahara Desert. It said the French academy had just awarded the writer and pilot, Antoine de Saint-Exupéry, their highest literary award for his autobiographical novel, *Land of Men*.

When I asked Señor Kurt about it, he said. "Saint-Exupéry is a famous pilot and journalist. He's been in Spain reporting on the civil war since 1936 for the Republicans. His most famous book is *The Little Prince*. You must read it if you ever get the chance.

I have never forgotten that conversation, or those three memorable days.

7

So I had become a Cárdenas orphan after all.

I can see the irony now. But at the time? No. I'd just turned fifteen and grieving was painful.

I was confused, particularly when Kurt and Frida left for Los Angeles and I was back at school with the others. I'd lost Mamá and Papá and with them my sense of belonging, my sense of direction towards a future I could look forward to.

My idea of a home with them had lost all meaning. No more postcards. No letters from Papá. Time had come to a mysterious and frightening standstill. I felt paralysed, as if the world whirling around me and unfurling into the future was leaving me frozen in its wake.

One hot summer afternoon not long after Kurt's departure, I deliberately tortured myself by swimming laps alone for what seemed pointless hours up and down President Cárdenas's swimming pool. He had taken a group of us out to his house with its wide shady verandas overlooking Lake Cuitzeo.

I didn't care whether I lived or drowned as I counted the tiles along the bottom.

My eyes stung in the warm chlorinated water.

There were one hundred and twenty-seven in each of thirty-five rows.

They were pale blue with dark blue spirals on them, like labyrinths, as if they'd been imprinted there by Ammonite fossils.

The sequence of numbers as I counted was eerily hypnotic. Each number following its predecessor measured out the flow of time, yet I felt dreamily outside the flow. I seemed out of touch with the normal world of change and consequence.

It was both comforting and terrifying, until President Cárdenas's wife, Mamá Amalia Solórzano herself, dived into the pool to convince me to end the session and join the others on the bus ride back to school.

During the next few months I often used to wander off on my own and walk around Morelia, unsure where I was going and what I was doing, or play my guitar in a quiet corner of the school yard, sometimes with my best friend Guillermo Reyes.

I was dazed and confused, but knew I had to rely on myself from then on. It took me the best part of the following year to regain my equilibrium and rebuild the confidence to map out my future."

By 1943, when I was turning eighteen and matriculating in my final year, the school in Morelia was running out of money and support.

The political situation was becoming complicated. Nationalist General Franco was the leader of Spain, and he had called on the Mexican Government to return the remaining children at the school to Spain.

The new President, Ávila Camacho, elected in 1940, agreed to ship us out. He was keen to wash his hands of us.

Fortunately for me and the others, Republican refugees were still pouring into Mexico. They saved the situation, by organising several boarding houses for us in Mexico City. So we moved into them and the school in Morelia was closed down.

At the same time, ex-President Cárdenas arranged a place for me and for Guillermo Reyes in UNAM, the *Universidad Autónoma de México*, in the engineering faculty, studying to become geological engineers—but there was one condition: we had six months' wait before the academic year began, and we both had to re-join the *Ejército Infantil de Cultura*, the Children's Cultural Army, and work for that time in the campaign across the country, stamping out illiteracy.

We'd been members of the Children's Army for the past two years at school.

In our spare time, we'd worked in Morelia, looking for kids and adults who couldn't read or write and wanted to learn. We spread the message that to become a true 'mestizo' Mexican, you had to be literate.

We worked in teams of ten or so, with a maestra in charge, to teach them how.

Even the primary school kids helped—the cleverer ones.

It was good fun, especially when Director López handed out 'Good Mexican' certificates at Friday assemblies to those who'd recorded five successful cases who were now basically literate. Some of us even got our names and photos into the Education Department SEP magazine.

Guillermo decided to work at his home in Durango, so I started working there with him at first.

Then we got a call from the teacher in Chihuahua City urgently requesting volunteers.

So I went.

9

In Chihuahua City, Mexico—*Friday, 30 April, 1943*, El Dia Del Niño, *Children's Day*

I clearly remember the day I joined the new team.

After running down the Calle Guadeloupe from my boarding house, I reached the Cathedral where we'd agreed to meet. I checked my watch and found I was half an hour late.

There were already six others sitting on the cathedral steps. Panting, and about to apologise for being late, I took off my sunglasses and glanced up at the cathedral clock. It was stuck on ten-nineteen, showing just under an hour and a quarter earlier.

"Hola, I'm Victor Serrano, from Morelia," I said, then pointed up at the clock. "I thought I was late, but it looks as if I'm early."

One of the young women looked up at me and laughed. She stood and lifted the book she was reading, her forefinger holding the page open.

"I'm Suré," she said. "So, you're early, not late, just because the cathedral clock tells the right time twice a day? If that's the case I have time to buy myself another *paleta* fruit icy pole."

A shock ran through me like a bolt of lightning.

Had we met before? Somewhere, somehow?

It was an otherworldly moment—and it was the same for her, she admitted to me later.

She was beautiful. Her face beneath her fringe was exquisitely shaped, her lively brown eyes captivating. Her thick black hair was drawn back in a long ponytail and it shone in the sunlight, displaying her profile as she looked down at the others. Her bronze skin glowed.

"Would anyone else like one?" she asked.

When no one answered, she handed me her book. "Can you keep my place for me, Víctor? What flavour do you like? Pineapple? Mango? Tamarind? Vanilla with almond flavouring, maybe?"

"Vanilla with almond flavouring sounds good," I said.

"I guessed as much. I like a man with good taste."

Before I could dip my free hand into my pocket for coins, she'd slipped off her sandals and darted away in her bright ruby-red blouse and long green skirt.

She weaved barefoot through the many colourful families milling around the balloon and piñata sellers on the Plaza de Armas.

I saw her sprinting past the roasting corncob braziers, almost upsetting the peanut seller as he cascaded a shower of what looked like salted and chilli nuts from an aluminium scoop held above his right shoulder into newspaper cones twisted into shape with his other hand.

She tore past the fresh papaya with sliced lemon stall and the mango, sugar cane and pineapple barrows, before disappearing behind two magicians surrounded by packs of rowdy children. A clown on stilts was among them. He was swaying on alternate legs high above their *oooohs* and *aaaahs*.

I caught another sudden glimpse of her beside the dazzling acrobat in a body-hugging silver costume. He was juggling five large Golden Delicious apples, taking alternate bites out of them, his hands as quick as striking snakes.

Beyond them all, I caught sight of her again, a flash of red and green, her black ponytail and scarlet ribbon flying from side to side as she glided across the grass before disappearing from sight behind the bandstand.

What just happened? Was she real? Will she reappear? I wondered.

My focus shifted to seven mariachi musicians in black and white playing a catchy Cri-Cri song in the shaded bandstand. The baritone singer at the microphone was dressed as a singing cricket in a lime and orange fancy dress. A row of empty Corona beer bottles glinted along the bandstand railing.

Then I looked down at her book, read the title and was stunned.

She was reading *The Little Prince*, by Antoine de Saint-Exupéry. It was the last thing I expected. I recalled the article in Kurt Lessing's news sheet and his advice—and there I was, four years later, holding that very book in my hands.'

When I read the title I knew my destiny was revealing itself to me.

I opened it and silently read the first words on the page Suré had reached.

"Aqui esta mi secreto. Es muy simple: Soló con el corazón se puede ver correctamente; lo que es esenciel es invisible a los ojos", "And now here is my secret. It's simple: It's only with the heart that one can see rightly; what is essential is invisible to the eye."

By the time I caught sight of Suré winding her way back towards me waving the two paletas, one scarlet, one white, I knew the quotation by heart.

When we moved into the shade of the cathedral and sat with our backs to the cool granite wall to enjoy the paletas, I surprised her by reciting the passage word perfect.

Six months later, when it was time for me to go back to Mexico City to enrol, I kissed her goodbye when her sister Ariché, our chaperone, wasn't looking.

Suré told me that moment beside the cathedral wall won her over. It was frozen in time at ten-nineteen, like the paletas that numbed our teeth.

The cathedral bells had been striking twelve in spite of the clock, and she'd barely heard me. Just as well I raised my voice and gave my destiny a helping hand.

I'd only known her for half an hour, but the moment was so precious it lasted for many lifetimes for both of us.

The memory of it is always accompanied by the rich taste of our paletas."

Pablo Picasso 'Guernica' – Courtesy Peter Eastland / Alamy stock photo

CHAPTER SIX

1

Back in Saucillo, Northern Mexico, April 1968

PAPÁ GAZED AT EACH of us for several long moments as if wondering how we'd responded to his story.

I didn't tell him an unbearable burst of shock had slammed across my chest when he'd told us Abu Xavier had been shot.

I heard Andrés gasp. 'No! You've never told us that before.'

"So… that's how I met your mamá," Papá said after a few moments, picking up the photo album again. "Everything I've told you today is a lot for you two to take in, but you must never believe Abu Xavier lost his life for nothing. I want to show you something special Kurt Lessing brought with him."

He opened the album to a plastic pouch at the back and withdrew a postcard-sized photo of a grey, black and white abstract painting. He held it out in front of us.

I had never seen it before.

"This is a copy of one of the most famous anti-war paintings in the world. It's a mural showing the bombing of Guernica." He indicated several features in turn. "See the screaming women, the gored horse and the flames? See the dismembered soldier and the bull's head?"

"And the dead baby," I said, pointing.

"And the dead baby, of course. It was painted by a famous Spanish artist, Pablo Picasso, in 1937." He hesitated. "Have either of you heard of him?"

"I have," Andrés said. "We've got some posters of his work up in the art classroom at school."

"Well, let me tell you, Abu Xavier's photos published in the newspapers inspired Picasso to paint his masterpiece. So you were right, Andrés. If not for the bombing of Guernica, I wouldn't be in Mexico and would never have met your mamá."

"In which case me and Alicia wouldn't exist," Andrés said.

"And everyone in the town would still be alive. Especially those children!" I said, as if participating in a strange game of Consequences whose rules I didn't yet understand. I sensed the powerful beating of my heart racing against my ribs and added breathlessly, "I wish they were."

"This will interest you both," Papá turned to another page in the album. "I have a photo here of Mamá with you, Alicia, a baby in her arms. Most of the photos are Abu Xavier's, but not this one. This is Tía Ariché's work, right down to the tinting."

He held the page open, but Andrés had a better view of it than I did, and I had to push him aside to see.

"Can you believe it?" Papá said. "Tía took it in black and white on the Kodak Brownie camera she was so proud of, before adding in the colours. This is your mamá. I'm sure you recognise her, Andrés?"

"Of course I do."

Suddenly tense, I looked down at my clenched fists as Andrés spoke.

"What do you remember most?" Papá asked.

"Oh, her running, of course. And her voice. Especially when she sang… and when she made me laugh."

I felt a sudden uncomfortable chill. It was alright for Andrés. I had no memory of her, so her absence became unbearably present once again. Her not being there was all I could recall, and I felt cheated.

The emptiness was agonising, and without warning, a paralysing thought crossed my mind. *Does Andrés blame me for Mamá's death? I've never asked him and he has never said so, but there's every chance he does. Especially since I arrived in the house the month Mamá disappeared.*

"She was good at all three," Papá commented. He gave me a sharp nudge with his elbow. "And that is you in the photo."

Neither of them noticed my distress as the piercing thought persisted, *Have I hurt Andrés just by being born?*

My mind raced as I leaned across for a closer look.

Andrés was ten years my senior. He'd been a hero to me since my infancy. I held him in awe and became his shadow, clearly often much to his annoyance. We both shared the tragedy of losing Mamá at an early age. It cemented our closeness more strongly than we understood, but he'd known her for a period of ten years. He was able to bring her to life more realistically than I could in my imagination.

That may be true, but what about me? Surely I miss her as much as he does.

He had hurt my feelings on more than one occasion when we were squabbling, and he insisted the grief he experienced at losing Mamá had to be deeper than mine.

"You never knew her," he used to say. "Not really. I did. So how can you say you miss her as much as me? You can't lose someone you never knew."

"How do you know?" I'd shout back. "Because I never knew her doesn't mean I miss her less than you. I was inside her for nine months, don't forget, and with her for a month after I was born. She was *never* there for me again. At least you have known her for ten years. Her death left a bigger hole in my life than you think."

I gritted my jaw and did my best to shut down my racing thoughts. I gazed down at myself half-hidden in the folds of her bright green dress. My back was to the camera as I nuzzled at her breast.

Concerned I'd be looking at a stranger, I was surprised to discover it wasn't the case, perhaps because she so closely resembled Tía Ariché. Her long black hair fell on each side of her face, framing it. Her eyes, which struck me as remarkably like Tía's, were dark and liquid yet bright with humour.

Despite her dark skin, Tíá had rouged her cheeks and tinted her lips, unnecessarily glamorising her, because to me, she was way beyond pretty. She was beautiful.

Looking at her with me in her arms, imagining myself drawing warm milk from her breast as my heart beat rapidly against hers, I concealed as best I could the confusion swirling through my mind.

It's bad enough me blaming myself for Mamá's death, but it's far worse suspecting Andrés may blame me too, perhaps along with others in the family. Even Papá? Surely not!

"No wonder you liked her," I managed to whisper, desperately quietening my mind.

"No wonder," Papá replied. "She took me by surprise on the cathedral steps when I was unprepared."

As I studied myself feeding at Mamá's breast, a wave of anguish overwhelmed me. *Mamá loved me then, as a mother does, with a mother's nurturing love that can never be replaced.*

Papá smiled. "Don't forget, she took one look at me and felt the same. Wouldn't you?"

"*Tú deseas,*" Andrés broke out laughing. "You wish."

"After a facelift, maybe?"

"Perhaps. And that's a big perhaps."

"Can I have the photo, Papá?" I whispered.

Papá did not hesitate. "Of course you can, if it's okay with Tía, but we'll keep it safe for you in here until you have an album or a photo wallet of your own."

2

He turned the page and showed us two more photographs of Guernica taken in a different part of the town.

In the foreground of the first, several buildings were facing a young leafy oak tree. They had escaped the bombing from the incoming waves of aircraft. Beyond them lay the town in ruins.

The second photo showed an ancient, blackened tree trunk standing protected in a cage of pillars, also untouched. The smoking ruins were visible beyond it.

"It looks as if time has stopped in one part of the town and is continuing in the other, as if two separate photographs, randomly ripped apart, have been joined together for dramatic effect," Papá said, running his finger along the jagged border between the ruins and the intact buildings. "On one side, the way things were, and on the other, the way things now are. Things we'll never forget."

He took a deep breath and I saw a tremor run across his shoulders.

"The oak trees are very special to us Basque Spaniards. The old tree trunk has a history stretching back to the fourteenth century. It's called the *Gernikako Arbola* and symbolises all the traditional freedoms of the Basque people.

"It represents our *eusko abertzaletasuna*, our sovereign nationhood. The younger tree was grown using an acorn from the latest in the line. Those buildings behind it are the Casa de Juntas, the Basque Government buildings."

I had little idea what he meant, but I loved the sounds of the words he'd just pronounced.

The complex music in the way he'd accentuated them.

The way the sounds became words carrying meaning.

How the words conjured images into existence in my mind: the *Gernikako Arbola*, the oak tree, so special to the Basque people.

I asked him to repeat them so I could whisper them to myself. He did, and we spent several delightful minutes echoing with one another until I'd learned them.

I spoke Spanish and Tarahumaran as fluently as could be expected of a seven-year-old turning eight, and these new Basque words fascinated me, even though I had trouble getting my tongue around them at first.

"We call the Basque language 'Euskara'," Papá said as he corrected me. "Now there's another Basque word for you."

He then said the living tree was so important its acorns were used to grow special seedlings—one to replace the current tree in case it died, others to send to Basque people who'd emigrated across the world.

He doubted we would qualify for one when I pleaded with him but, "*Nunca sabes*, you never know. If you and Andrés send a special letter worded just right to the soft-hearted nurseryman, he might convince the current *lehendakari*, President Jesús de Leizaola, to allow him to send you one."

"We won't hold our breath." Andrés said as I voiced the new word I'd just heard.

While Papá continued talking to Andrés about the bombing, I busied myself writing out my new Basque words with a red crayon onto a blank page torn from the back of one of his sketch pads. I interrupted him now and then to spell them out.

"I'll go to Guernica one day and hug that tree," I overheard Andrés say.

"It will, without doubt, hug you back."

Looking up from my completed list, I said, "I'll come with you."

I held my list out to Papá.

"*Lehend-a-kari*, not *lehend-i-kari*," he corrected me after a moment. "Otherwise, it's excellent, Alicia."

"*Lehendakari*," I repeated after him, "The Basque president."

"So the word conjures up an image of him in your mind? Isn't that a miracle?"

"Of course it does. *Lehendakari, es su palabra*, that's his word," I said, looking down at my list. "That's what words do. They tell you everything you need to know."

"About the person?"

"About everything in the world… it doesn't matter what," I said slowly and shyly, stumbling over my words as I struggled to explain the mysterious relationship between sounds, words and meanings, between an image and the language describing it.

I broke off and began carefully sketching a green oak tree beside the words *Gernikako Arbola*.

"*Es su palabra*," Andrés teased me, his voice sarcastic. "That's conjuring for you, my little miracle worker."

He leaned across and threatened to flick the top of my crayon, but I jerked it away and jabbed the pointy end into his ribs.

"Serves you right," Papá said when he complained. "Lesson one in good relations with a señorita. Never disturb her when she's concentrating on her work."

When I'd corrected the list and completed the picture, I handed it back to Papá for a final check. He nodded as he read the words and was about to return it when he stopped abruptly.

"What's this word?" He pointed at the last word on the list I'd added as an afterthought. "Is it meant to be *septicaemia*?"

"Yes."

"And it tells you everything you need to know?"

"Yes, I think so."

"Do you want the Basque spelling for it?"

"Yes, please."

He took the red crayon and corrected my spelling, before handing me the list and giving me a tight and silent hug lasting for way longer than I'd expected—so long it seemed as though Mamá herself was reaching out to me through him, thrilling me and bringing me close to tears as I returned the hug.

I ran my eye down my list, sounding each strange new word in my mind, learning them by heart—and then I suddenly recalled a word Papá had used when telling his story.

"Papá, what's *Kristallnacht*? Is it English?"

"It's German. The Night of Broken Glass. When the German Nationalists smashed the windows in Jewish shops and houses in many cities in Germany and set them on fire."

I made a separate column with my crayon and wrote 'German' across the top. "How do you spell it?"

"Enough is enough. German now? You're going overboard."

"No. How do you spell it?"

Papá gazed at me, bemused, his eyebrows raised. "Really?"

I gave him a winning smile. "Really."

"Trust you to insist!" he said, as he spelled it out and I wrote it down.

3

Papá leaned down and picked up the cigar case from between his feet.

"Now we come to another chain of coincidences that led me to becoming a geologist at the Naica mine... this collection of rocks."

He opened the case and tipped out a handful of rocks, each wrapped in thick tissue. He spread them with his right hand as Andrés and I shifted our positions to get a better view.

He picked one up and unwrapped a cluster of light pink selenite crystals. He placed it to one side. "You've seen this type of crystal before," he said.

"Abu Cerrildo's got lots of them," Andrés said. "Mostly clear white."

"From the Cave of Swords. For the chess pieces he carves," I added.

"This one here is special," Papá said.

It was the first of its kind he'd ever seen, he explained. It belonged to his friend Guillermo, who had several in his collection.

"His were pale green, white and pale pink to red, similar to this one. Like the colours in the Mexican flag. Guillermo told me they came from the Naica mine in Chihuahua, over the border from his home in Durango. It's beautiful, don't you think? The first time he showed it to me I knew I had to have it, so we swapped. Guillermo struck a tough bargain—three of my sandstone fossils in exchange. Three for one. He always was *nariz dura*, hard-nosed."

His grin became a chuckle.

"But at least he paid for my Lulú lemon sodas next time we went to the cinema. Twice. To thank me."

As he unwrapped the other rocks, some embedded with fossils, he told us he used to go on long walks with Abu Xavier when he was photographing landscapes and sunsets before the civil war. In the Ordesa Valley and on the slopes of Mt Perdido in Basque country, in the western Pyrenees.

"I found these up there," he said. "Papá started taking me with him when I was four years old. I'd be riding on his shoulders most of the time or looking for salamanders and tadpoles in the rivers with Mamá when he was photographing the rock walls and waterfalls."

He held each rock out in turn, describing the black coiled nummulite fossils, the fan-like alveolina and the barely visible patterns of orbitoid shells set in the flat shards of sandstone.

He saved what he called his pride and joy for last.

It was a fist-sized ochre-coloured nodule embedded in grey limestone. It was a silex sponge crystallised into quartz over many millions of years, he explained.

Holding it up to the window he turned it this way and that, the sunlight flaring in amber sparks from the microcrystals like a mini chandelier.

"Imagine it growing on the seabed long before the Pyrenee Mountains were formed." He looked up and smiled. "When I first took it home, I used to picture myself diving in the ocean long, long ago while it was still alive, taking underwater photographs of it growing among others. And here we are, sitting in Saucillo, admiring it and listening to its story. It's like I'm reading to you from a book. We each have our story, including this sponge. Isn't that a miracle?"

"So your rocks are books, and your collection is a library?" Andrés asked.

"That's what Papá used to call it—my *Biblioteca de la Naturaleza Rocosa*. My own Nature's Library of Rocks, recording the history of the earth itself."

"That's why you became a geologist," I said.

"It is. And if I hadn't, I wouldn't have joined the Children's Cultural Army and worked in Chihuahua City, where I met your mamá. Now *that* was a chain of coincidences."

"And we wouldn't be here to prove you did." Andrés burst out laughing. "I was right. You did have rocks in your head… and still do."

"And you inherited my genes."

"So did I," I said.

"Ah, but your rocks are *words* and you must never stop collecting them."

We sat in silence, rewrapping the rocks as Papá packed them carefully back into the cigar case. He closed the lid and tapped out two unexpected drumrolls with all his fingers on it, before replacing it in the suitcase and closing it.

Then he stood, hoisted it to the top of the wardrobe, and ushered us back out into the lounge.

Andrés running – Courtesy FC Italy / Alamy stock photo

CHAPTER SEVEN

1

DURING 1967, ANDRÉS AND I often used to sweat alongside our Tarahumaran grandfather Cerrildo, helping him clean his 1956 Golden Hawk Studebaker. It was parked in the driveway of our house in Saucillo.

The car was a sight to behold. It was Abu's pride and joy. I can still see the excitement in his unusual almond-shaped dark brown eyes, his smile with a single silver crown standing out. The creases in his leathery skin deepened as his smile widened and he pushed back the brim of his sweat-stained white Stetson hat and described the car's mechanical qualities for anyone prepared to listen.

"Four gears and overdrive on the steering column gearshift," he loved to boast, "and she's powered by a *trescientos cincuanta y dos pulgada cúbica*, a 352 cubic-inch, OHV Packard V8. Would you like to take a look?"

He'd have the bonnet open and up in a flash, the engine block cracking like a shotgun as it cooled.

"Here she is, *mi bestia gruñona*, my growling beast. Naught to sixty kilometres an hour in eight seconds. What do you think?"

We hosed down and polished the two-tone orange and cream bodywork and steam-cleaned the engine and chassis, especially after Andrés's monthly marathon training runs in preparation for the 1968 Mexico City Olympic trials.

They were now a year away.

On the weekends, Andrés used to run alongside the car for three or four hours over forty-two dusty kilometres on the gravel road from the right-hand turn off at the Conchos overpass. The road ran westwards to the Naica mine where Papá was the Chief Geologist and Abu Cerrildo worked as a security guard.

Or we'd drive south towards Camargo on Highway 45D, with Andrés running along the verge. The bitumen cut through shady pecan and alfalfa orchards, and past green fields of jalapeño, maize and groundnuts.

I distinctly remember one Saturday afternoon in October that year, when Abu first pushed back his seat. He made room for me to sit in front of him and learn to steer while he changed gears and worked the pedals.

I was seven years old.

I fought to suppress my giggling excitement as my arms struggled to manage the car's unaccustomed weight. Such responsibility. Such trust.

He had the windows down and rhythmic mariachi music blaring as he shouted instructions at Andrés right beside my ear, deafening me.

"Glide, boy! Glide! Keep your feet close to the ground, each stride fluent and economical. Save your energy. Elbows in, and hands in line with your hips until you're sprinting, and then you wait for my instructions!"

It took me several kilometres to get the knack of the steering wheel.

Whenever a distant cloud of rising dust signalled oncoming traffic, I resumed my seat and became Andrés's helper again. I passed a water bottle out through the passenger window, or one of Tía Ariché's special chia energy bars when he needed it as he slipped along, his hands held low, his feet barely leaving the ground as though he was skating on ice, his clipped stride quick but deceptive in length.

"Just under two metres, *nieto*," Abu had told him earlier, after measuring both our strides as we'd loped around the circuit lined with pencil pines in our backyard. "You'll have to build up your stride length when you're sprinting. It will come. You're only sixteen."

"Almost seventeen," Andrés corrected him.

"I beg your pardon, seventeen next month. You are filling out, I grant you. The weights and gymnastics are doing you good. And kayaking with Alicia on the Conchos River and Rosetilla dam, of course."

"Not to mention his favourite food he scoffs down when we're running up at Cerocahui," I added, recalling Tía Ariché's mouth-watering tortilla, beans and squash and her chilles rellenos with three eggs and tomato salsa.

"Yes, her recipes are to *die* for." Abu closed his eyes and sucked in his lips to kiss the four fingertips of his right hand. "Like her second-to-none goat meat tacos *de cabeza* I can't resist."

"They're all so filling, but greedy guts here, he always goes back for seconds. Even for *chica* Camila's cooking here in Saucillo," I added with a grin, referring to the basic but always tasty meals our housemaid was teaching me to cook after school.

"And sometimes thirds," Andrés said proudly.

"*Comes lo suficiente para engordar una palanca.* You eat enough to fatten a crowbar," Abu commented, patting him on the back.

2

Andrés often seemed lost in a meditative daydream as he ran those longer distances beside the car.

I used to wonder what he was thinking about.

Was his mind blank as he counted the kilometres slipping by? Was he noticing changes in the passing scenery? The clouds changing shape in the upper winds? The sun climbing through the big sky, rendering it a paler blue?

Or was he concentrating on enduring the pain he was experiencing until it became second nature?

Or maybe imagining creative new floor plans and designs for the houses and buildings I'd watched him drawing in his bedroom at home. He'd been doing it since he enrolled in architecture as a compulsory arts option to his Physical Education degree at the National Polytechnic Institute in Mexico City next year.

From then on, when I wasn't busy steering, I'd look out for a change in his expression signalling he was about to accelerate to a light canter or an occasional sprint, before easing back after a minute or two.

He'd give a sudden, determined frown as he rose to the challenge. He'd fluently lengthen stride, his arms driving his legs to a higher knee-lift. He seemed to float across the ground, his upper body perfectly balanced. Geronimo would look up with an occasional approving bark as he raced along beside him like his shadow.

"What do you think about when you're running faster?" I asked him once. "What goes through your mind?"

"I must decide in a split second whether I'm a frightened hare caught in the headlights of anyone who's going to chase me down when I overtake them on the back straight—or an Olympic champion with the killer instinct, like Billy Mills in Tokyo in 1964. Then nobody's going to catch me once I kick in and take the lead. I'm training myself to feel I'm so fit and strong I'll grind them into the dust after turning into the home straight."

He gave the characteristic burst of laughter I loved to hear and always shared, even though I may not laugh out loud.

"The other thing I do once I've changed gears is recite a poem to myself. It has the perfect rhythm for running hard and its meaning speaks to me. The school coach found it for the athletics team. It's called *If*, by an English poet, Rudyard Kipling. He was a runner too, so he knew what he was writing about. You want to hear the last verse?"

"Of course."

"Si puedes llenar el minuto implacable
Con sesenta segundos de distancía recorrida,
Tuya es la Tierra y todo lo que hay en ella,
Y—lo que es más—serás un Hombre, hijo mío!
If you can fill the unforgiving minute
With sixty seconds' worth of distance run,
Yours is the Earth and everything that's in it,
And—which is more—you'll be a Man, my son!'

He nodded proudly. "Once I'm up and running, with overdrive still in reserve, I keep repeating, *Serás un hombre, hijo mío, serás un Hombre!* as I race towards a target at the side of the road—a tree, a light pole or a sign a hundred or a hundred and fifty metres away. Before I reach it, I switch on the turbochargers and sprint the last thirty or forty metres flat out until I dip through the tape."

When I heard that, the first time he raised his pace I teased him by shouting the refrain through the window.

I used words of my own.

"Serás un hombre, mi hermano! You'll be a man, my brother! *Serás un hombre, pero no por un tiempo todavía,* but not for a long time yet."

"*Dices tú, ardilla.* Says you, chipmunk," he shouted back.

There were times when he slowed his pace to recharge his batteries, as he put it. He'd signal with his left hand, and I'd open the door and join him.

I'd jog for anything up to a kilometre with him, careful not to trip over Geronimo as he bounded up to give me a welcome lick, before he picked up the pace once more and left me struggling behind him.

I loved it.

So much so that running became my other passion, after words and language. I knew I had a talent for both, as both came naturally to me. I spoke both Tarahumaran and Spanish well by the time I was five and I was learning English at school and extending my Basque vocabulary with Papá when he had time to respond to my pestering.

As well as running with Andrés, I also ran in teams with other Tarahumaran girls my age and older when I was up at at Cerocahui.

We'd chase a wooden *ariweta* hoop rolled between us with our sticks beside the river at Urique; or we'd run through the scrubby pines and oaks along the crest of the Copper Canyon for as long as we enjoyed it.

We were never conscious of the time, but revelled in the sheer exhilaration of the sport.

We learnt to perfect our skills, moving as lightly and efficiently across the rocky ground as our developing bodies allowed. When we watched the older women also running, we were aware we'd be doing so for a lifetime—perfecting the art of running and living up to our preferred indigenous name of Rarámuri, the light-footed ones.

And uncannily, through it all, I was conscious of Mamá, wondering if she was watching me and appreciating everything I did, as though I was doing it all as much for her as for myself.

Which of course I was.

3

Another thing I loved doing with Andrés was paddling one of the two small marine ply kayaks Abu Cerrildo made for us the previous year. They were smaller versions of his sea-going kayak, which he used on the Rosetilla Dam whenever we went there for picnics.

We helped him build them in his work shed in the back garden.

He started with both frames upside down on what he called his Pegasus sawhorses. I say we helped, but what I mean is we did our best to curb our enthusiasm and not get in his way or test his patience.

On a good day we'd hand him his tools, or screws, nails and glue when he needed them as he worked. He'd be whistling between his teeth. Occasionally he'd shove his hat back to scratch his forehead when things were going wrong, before swearing under his breath, apologising and making us laugh.

"Don't tell me you heard that. If you did, don't let me hear you repeat it."

Once he'd covered the frames with the plywood panels of the hulls, we spent several afternoons painting them. Then he left us to our own devices. I chose a brilliant orange and Andrés a navy blue. When they were sealed and dry, we launched them on the Conchos River in full flood at the bottom of the garden.

It was such an adventure I could barely hold my excitement in check!

"Using these will give your upper bodies the strength you need for your running," Abu told us, as he waded out waist-deep and helped us into the wooden seat.

He strapped our legs in place, and warned us, "I have strict rules. You'll use them as part of your training program and sometimes on a day off, but only if I say so. You must never use them when I am not around to watch you."

He patted the safety jacket he'd shown us how to wear. "You will always wear one of these. When you are used to the kayaks I will take you to the Rosetilla Dam with mine, and we can all paddle around it."

Abu was so right.

Within a year, Andrés was broader in the shoulders and much stronger, and I was wirier, fitter and running faster.

In Mexico City, early December 1967
On a hot Sunday afternoon, in the foothills of the Paso de Cortés, in Zoquiapan National Park, I clutched Papá's hand, my heart thumping.

The leading group of runners bounded past us for the second time. They'd reached the halfway point in the eight-kilometre cross-country race for senior schoolboys.

Andrés was among them. He was running third or fourth. I caught our pre-agreed signal—he lifted a forefinger to his right eyebrow. It told us he was feeling good, with plenty in the tank, all high-octane fuel waiting for the spark, as he described it.

I checked the stopwatch—thirteen minutes, thirty-five seconds and counting. Close to the national record pace for Mexican junior boys aged eighteen and below.

From the slope overlooking the course, we could see the line of runners as they laboured up the next hill. Some were now falling back, several walking at the rear, a handful stretching away at the front.

Andrés was in the mix, standing out in his brilliant blue and white Saucillo High School colours. Then he disappeared over the top and into the pine plantations.

Clouds spilled across the crests of the two nearby volcanoes, Iztaccíhuatl and Popocatépetl, and the sky was a blinding sunlit blue.

Stratospheric winds were wiping away the chalky trail of a barely visible silver aircraft streaking across from east to west.

Has it just taken off from Benito Juárez airport in Mexico City? Are others lined up on the runway about to follow? Will their white trails entertain me with a heavenly game of tres en raya, *noughts and crosses, emblazoned across the sky?* I wondered.

I began imagining where I'd place my marks.

"Here they come!" Papá yelled, peering through his binoculars. "Just two of them. No, three."

I craned my neck to see, then fought my way to the front through the other spectators. Their conversations were rising to a crescendo of cheers, my screams among them.

Andrés and a taller runner, dressed in black, powered down the long slope beyond the trees towards us. They were running shoulder to shoulder. A third runner was struggling a distant thirty metres behind them.

A hundred and fifty metres from the finish, as though he was propelled by an invisible rubber cord stretching between my willing mind and his, Andrés took a step to his right.

Within several arm-pumping, smoothly accelerating strides, he gained a five-metre lead and slowly extended it, before he ducked through the tape.

In the last thirty metres of the race, the number 11 on his chest flapped upwards in his slipstream. I saw beneath it through my excitement and my tears the Saucillo High School badge on full display—*el correcamino*, the roadrunner.

Andrés is a roadrunner, but he's no Mexican chicken! The joke ran through my mind. *Eso es tan irónico, that's so ironic.*

Irony was a fascinating new abstract word in my vocabulary. Papá had taught me its meaning recently and I was struggling to understand it. Particularly tragic irony.

Papá suggested that Mamá surrendering her life in exchange for mine was a good example. It gave the impression that cosmic forces had shaped my destiny in an unexpected and tragic way.

When I checked the stopwatch in my sweaty hand, I realised I'd forgotten to press the button. I quickly did so, only to discover I'd added half a minute to Andrés's time. The official timekeeper later confirmed before the medal presentation he'd run the course in a new national junior record of twenty-seven minutes and five-point-four seconds.

"It was Billy Mills who helped me win," Andrés confided to us on the journey home. "He won the ten thousand metres in Tokyo at the last Games and he coached me all the way."

"What? Was he speaking to you in Oglala Lakota with someone translating for you into Tarahumaran?" I asked.

Papá gave a burst of laughter. "Trust you to know he was speaking Oglala Lakota."

"Well, that's his tribe," I replied defensively. "I read it on the poster up in Andrés's bedroom. Jim Thorpe on the other poster is a Sac and Fox. He speaks Algonquin."

Papá turned back to Andrés. "What advice did Billy give you?"

"When we came down the slope to the finishing line, it was like I was running with him on the last lap in Tokyo. The Tunisian, Mohammed Gammoudi, shoved his way through the gap between him and the Australian Ron Clarke to take the lead. He chased them both around the turn into the home straight. Then he stepped to the right, just like I did today, and blasted past to win the gold."

"Just like you did," I said admiringly.

"You recall all that from the film of the race?" Papá asked.

"Remember I told you about Señor Valentin, the German coach who's visiting us during the year of the Cultural Olympiad? He showed us the film at school. The last lap. Three times. He was pointing out how rough it can get on the track, how we have to avoid getting boxed in, and what to do if we are."

"You did well today," Papá said. "We're proud of you. The Olympic trials are next. Will you compete if your win today qualifies you?"

"If I get an invitation, maybe yes."

"No maybes, Andrés," I broke in. "Just a simple yes."

Two weeks later, we learned that his win, along with other times he'd recorded, had earned him an invitation to run in the ten thousand metres at the Mexican Olympic Trials.

5

In Saucillo, Northern Mexico, Sunday, 21 April, 1968

The Olympic trials for the Mexican team were televised on a late evening, a week after the Easter celebrations.

I was at home in Saucillo.

I carried the loose wiring and the aerial, while Abu Cerrildo lifted his black and white television out to his worktable on the back veranda.

I climbed up into the pistachio tree and hoisted the aerial into the upper branches above the roofline of the house. I lashed it in position when Abu, fiddling with the controls, shouted that reception was as clear as he could manage.

I climbed down as he adjusted the volume. The *Telesistema Mexicano* sports announcer's voice was commenting on a track event.

I leapt to the ground and rushed to Abu's side to check— the one hundred and ten metres hurdles for men had just finished. I glanced at the program. We had an hour to wait before Andrés ran the most important race of his young life.

He had enrolled for the February intake of students at the IPN, the *Instituto Polytécnico Nacional* in Mexico City, and we hadn't seen him since his departure. Papá had taken a week's leave to support him, even though he was not allowed to enter the Olympic stadium to watch the race.

Abu, the housemaid Camila and I settled into our chairs when the ten thousand metre runners were called to their marks.

It was impossible to distinguish them in the growing twilight and on the steady long shot taken, I guessed, through a camera stationed on the stadium roof.

Earlier events had involved closer cameras strategically placed around the stadium. We'd watched the muscles twitch in a tangle of sprinting legs one minute, a high jumper's distorted features as he sailed over the bar the next, or tracked a discus spinning high through the air across the stadium.

I was tense. I searched for Andrés but did not recognise him, as twenty or so small, shadowy figures shuffled into a curved line at the start.

There was a short delay, before the crack of the pistol set them off.

The bunched pack rocketed into the back straight, runners jostling for position before settling into pairs and single file down the back straight for the first time. Then the pace eased into a fluid stride as they came to the end of the first lap.

The field official turned the lap counter down to a number it was impossible to read, but I knew it was twenty-three more to run.

Who is who? Where is Andrés?

Multiple bulbs in the four floodlight towers overhead were glowing but refusing to fire up. For three laps the camera angle didn't change and the shell of the stadium darkened further… until the floodlights flared alight, each with a startling explosive crackle.

The runners now stood out as brilliant as day.

And Andrés? *There* he was—running freely in tenth position, looking comfortable.

The six floodlights shining on his body cast multiple shadows across the lanes, tracking every footfall.

José Garcia, who I'd seen in one of Andrés's *World Sports* magazines, was six or seven metres in the lead.

I imagined Papá following the race on his colour television in his Mexico City hotel—the white lines clear against the reddish tan of the rubberised tartan track, the deep green of the infield grass, the state colours of the runners' vests and shorts: Sinaloa scarlet, Jalisco orange, Chiapas black and yellow, Yucatán green, and Andrés in his Chihuahua silken blue,

He was running well, still in the middle of the field.

With ten laps to go, Andrés was holding his midfield position.

A leading group, including Garcia, Juan Martínez and Pablo Garrido, played a game of catch me if you can, threatening to draw away.

When the camera angle switched to a bird's eye view, the distant figures circling the track were too small and mesmerising for me to follow.

My attention was drawn instead to the stairway leading up to the Olympic cauldron. I decided to count the steps and imagined running up them, carrying the Olympic torch—ten grey steps between iridescent pink banisters per lap, ten laps to go.

Each time the leader passed the halfway point down the back straight, I'd sprint up another ten. I imagined I was running up the steps on an Aztec or Mayan pyramid, to see how close to the cauldron I'd be at the finish. Then I'd climb the rest and light the flame to celebrate Andrés winning.

After ninety-three steps I'd reached the summit.

My stomach was churning, and I was gasping for breath in my imagination.

Then I stood beside the cauldron, panting, the torch raised in my right hand.

I watched the start of the final lap, the camera angle switching back to close-up.

I had a trackside view as it followed Juan Martínez, leading, with four runners chasing him at the bell. Mario Saldivar was his closest challenger… and Andrés was still in eighth position, the length of the home straight behind them.

I was overwhelmed as Andrés passed the bell for the last lap.

Does it sound to him as it does to me, like the Chihuahua cathedral bell striking twelve for Mamá and Papá when they were nineteen and met for the first time on the cathedral steps in 1943?

He ran the bend into the final lap, digging deep.

His stride was long, but he was not yet at full sprint.

He was beautiful to watch, running smoothly and fluently as he cruised past another runner in the back straight and another as he turned for home. He held his form and gathered gazelle-like speed over the last thirty metres in a controlled sprint, before dipping through the finish in sixth position.

I leaned across to light the cauldron for him, sobbing with delight and pride.

Was it Billy Mills whispering to him in Oglala Lakota who inspired him to run so well, or Jim Thorpe in Algonquin this time?

Either way, it was a North American Indian sharing his secrets with a Central American Rarámuri Indian.

"*Sexto!*" Abu shouted. "Sixth!"

He sat shaking his head, looking down at the stopwatch in his trembling hand.

After a deep breath, "In thirty minutes and forty-eight point four seconds by this watch. And he was making ground on Martínez and the others in the last lap. He gained at least ten metres. Did you see him?"

"He was brilliant."

"He may have missed out on a place in the team this time, but you wait until the Munich Games." He gave me a hug and choked the breath out of me, before releasing me with a lopsided grin, his eyebrows arched upwards, his silver tooth flashing, "He couldn't have done it without our coaching could he, *nieta?* You and me both."

"You and me and Geronimo, Abu," I said, "and the Studebaker, of course."

"Ah, *mi bestia gruñona.* We must not forget her. Or the kayaks."

"And Camila's special nutritious diet," I added, placing my arm across our shy maid's plump shoulders as she ducked away. A blush rose beneath her olive skin to the silver coronet of her hair, pinned back with a large tortoiseshell comb.

I did not tell them I'd climbed the steps to light the cauldron, striving upwards with one goal in mind—to reach the top, determined to succeed without a backward step.

To do it on my own and please Mamá.

And I'd known for certain I'd concentrate on a *two*-lap race from then on. Just the two. No further. One lap cruising to the bell, the next a sprint to the finish.

Another twenty-two laps, like Andrés? Out of the question. The eight hundred metres two lap race, that will suit me, thank you very much.

6

Six months later, the hallway telephone shrilled while Camila was preparing breakfast. The rich warm smells of coffee, *pan dulce* sweetbread and eggs Mexicana spread through the house, carrying with them the sharper whiff of salsa made with pickled jalapeños, onion and tomatoes.

The phone went quiet before it shrilled again.

I was dressed for school but still barefoot, my mouth watering and stomach rumbling.

I slammed my bedroom door behind me and rushed down the corridor towards the dining room to answer it. I collided with Papá, who'd left the table to do the same. We both apologised and laughed, but as I retreated, I heard him raise his voice.

It was so rare for him I froze.

"Enough, Andrés. *Enough!*" I flinched when he roared, "How many times have I warned you not to get involved?"

He glanced angrily in my direction, sending me a hurtful dismissive wave as he growled, "I don't care what your peers are doing."

I slid shut the dining room door before joining Abu and Tío Guillermo at the table.

Tío was visiting us from Mexico City, where he was UNAM's Professor of Mining Engineering. The three of us sat in surprised silence, Papá's voice hoarse with concern and anger reaching us during the next fifteen minutes. Bursting with curiosity and straining to hear, I couldn't decipher the conversation.

It ended when he slammed down the phone.

"You and I were both mistaken, it seems," he said when he joined us at the table, angrily dragging back his chair.

He snatched up his serviette before facing me.

"Running is not his only passion, he tells me. Politics is a part of student life. A part of *his* student life, he insists, from now on. He was one of the three hundred thousand in the silent march to the Zócalo Square last Friday. He thinks it was some sort of holy pilgrimage. Who knows what he's risking if the authorities find out? They'd have had spies everywhere in the crowd, mixing with the students. With cameras, no doubt."

"Is this the first time he's taken part in the student rallies?' Tío Guillermo asked.

He swivelled his broad shoulders towards Papá. The taut brown skin on his shaved head shone as if polished and the tendons bulged in his bull neck. The silver hair curling among the black on his chest showed in the inverted triangle of the open collar on his denim shirt.

"Apparently not. He joined both marches last month as well, he tells me. He was there when they took down the tricolour and raised the anarchist flag, for God's sake. How disrespectful and dangerous was that?"

"Students will be students," Tío Guillermo said, wiping his mouth with his serviette.

I was stunned.

We'd watched the TV on Tuesday, 27 August, when the leaders of the huge crowd of students, teachers and workers of various unions who'd filled the Constitución Plaza had defiantly raised the revolutionary flag on the flagstaff.

"It's red below the diagonal and pitch-black above it," Abu had whispered to me when I'd asked as it rose up the mast. The breeze displayed it in black and white on his television set.

I'd been shocked as several light armoured cars, mounted with machine guns, driving three and four abreast, had driven through the crowd to disperse them. The granaderos riot police and a battalion of armed soldiers were in support. Live rounds had been fired, occasional bullets ricocheting from the surrounding buildings Showers of pulverised brick sprayed across the crowd.

And Andrés had been there!

A fortnight later, we'd watched the news again as busloads of government bureaucrats and public servants were driven to the Zócalo Square to take part in a rival demonstration supporting the government.

The granaderos offloaded them and forced them to raise the national flag back on the flagpole.

Reluctant to participate, they'd been satirically baaing like sheep as the enforced show of support for President Díaz Ordaz backfired.

"We won't lose our tickets to the Olympics, will we?" I blurted out across the table.

It was the first anxious thought that crossed my mind.

Andrés's sixth position in the trials had earned him a place on the reserve listing for the Mexican Olympic team and with it, four complimentary tickets for him and his family to attend the Games on any two days of our choosing.

We'd examined the track and field program and selected Tuesday and Wednesday, 15 and 16 October.

"I'd hate not to go. I've been looking forward to it for so long," I said.

"Never mind the Olympics," Papá snapped. "It's the least of our worries. I don't want to see Andrés arrested and imprisoned for God knows what offence."

"Or disappeared," Abu murmured, "like in the past. Remember the railway workers' strikes in 1958? Many strikers were arrested and never seen again. And the doctors struck for better conditions three years ago and were arrested. Same unforgivable story."

"Remember them?" Tío Guillermo frowned. "How could we forget? Demetrio Vallejo is still in prison, for God's sake. Eleven and a half years. For daring to speak up and organise the railway strikes. Sedition, they called it. Other union leaders like him were thrown into the Gulf of Mexico from helicopters, according to the rumours. Dead or alive. Who knows?"

"It's all true," Abu said. "Where's the justice?"

Then they all looked at me as if they'd just remembered I was there. In the tense silence Papá put a reassuring hand on my arm.

"Relax, *mijita*. Take no notice. This is men's talk, that's all. People sometimes do things to harm each other, but we'll make sure you and Andrés are safe. Come, put your shoes on and get your backpack. I'll drive you to school. You're twenty minutes late."

Take no notice? How can I take no notice? I was too appalled to reply.

I looked back at Papá, my mind racing as the silence lengthened and I stood to go back to my bedroom.

Everyone at school had been talking about the strikes and daily violence for months, some more hysterically than others.

Every new demonstration undertaken by school and university students in Mexico City and across the country, each more dramatic and revolutionary than the last, seemed to mark another crucial social and cultural turning point in our anxious young lives.

As I put my shoes on, my mind recalled some of the incidents.

The fights between vocational and private school students on 22 July, brutally broken up by the granaderos.

The demonstrations on 26 July by university students of the IPN Polytechnic in support of the vocational schools—Andrés among them, I discovered later, to my dismay. Days of rioting and school strikes followed, with buses smashed and set alight in the streets—and then the granaderos used a bazooka, of all things, to blast open the carved front door of the Idelfonso Preparatory School and dragged out rioters who'd taken refuge inside.

And the peaceful march of fifty thousand students and unionists on 1 August, led by the rector of the UNAM, Javier Barros Sierra, protesting at the heavy-handed tactics of the granaderos.

And worst of all the silent march we'd talked about at breakfast.

I will never forget the images on TV when it ended after sunset. Thousands of students held up burning rolled-up newspapers and pamphlets to illuminate their faces. Their mouths were sealed with black crosses of masking tape.

That was followed by brutal running battles during September between students and the granaderos, supported now by the full firepower of the army and air force helicopter gunships, as they occupied the various university campuses. The Government was determined to stamp out the unrest before the end of the month.

President Díaz Ordaz resolved to save the Olympic Games at whatever cost.

They were due to start on 12 October.

Olympic Games 1968 – Granaderos crushing the student demonstrations –
Student CNH cartoon / La Grafica Del '68

CHAPTER EIGHT

1

In Mexico City, 1 October, 1968

WHEN PAPÁ AND I joined Tío Guillermo at the Chihuahua City airport to fly to Mexico City for the Games, he said, "Things are getting much worse. They could go either way. Did you see the news? IOC President Brundage has given Díaz Ordaz a final warning. Control the students or he will cancel the Games."

Papá slowly shook his head. "Or transfer them to Los Angeles, I heard. God forbid."

"Knowing Ordaz as we do, he may see Brundage's threat as permission to crack down even harder on the students. So much for the peaceful Olympics."

"Touch wood our flight won't be wasted," Papá said.

Papá and Tío Guillermo were both putting the finishing touches to their mining display as part of the Cultural Olympiad, the year-long international cultural and economic program organised along with the Games.

The program was designed to show how technically advanced and progressive modern Mexico had become.

I was excited by the prospect of escaping school for a fortnight and helping them.

Tío Guillermo had arranged for us to stay with him and his wife, Tía Sofia, in their unit on the fourth floor of the Chihuahua building beside the Plaza de las Tres Culturas.

Just over two hours later, I was in the window seat beside Papá as the plane descended.

I was thrilled by the hazy spread of the city as the plane banked sideways to the left, dipping with unnerving vibrations in the seats and along the wings. Then I found myself peering up at the pale blue cloudless sky across the sheet of quivering aluminium on the wing as it turned back, angling to the right as we levelled off and skimmed closer to the buildings and streets.

They stretched out of view in all directions.

As we slowed in preparation for landing, we flew across a huge oval building squatting beneath us like a giant armadillo. Sunlight flashed from the scale-like cones in the copper sheathing of its roof.

Beside it, I made out six tall, bright yellow pillars and a magenta-coloured seventh. Shaped like polyhedrons, they transformed magically into seven stars in an elongated formation as we glided directly overhead and I looked down on them from above.

Tío Guillermo leaned across Papá and pointed. "That's the constellation of Ursa Major, and next to it the new Sports Palace for the Basketball," he said.

Papá had allowed me to bring Abu Xavier's old Leica camera with me on the trip.

I took my first colour photograph of the seven stars below and the roof of the Sports Palace.

Moments later, we flew across a small rectangular lake. Its surface was a glassy silver green. I prepared to photograph the plane's reflection as it flashed across, but it was too quick for me.

"That's the Nabor Carillo," Tío said, nodding at the lake as the runway rushed towards us.

The wheels squealed on concrete and the engines roared as we landed, their reverse thrust slowing us before we taxied towards the terminal buildings.

We disembarked and entered the airport concourse.

The ceiling above us was decorated with spectacular balloons of different sizes and rainbow colours, patterned with the psychedelic Mexico 1968 logo and other Olympic icons.

Andrés was standing at the entrance.

When I saw him, I took off at a run and sprinted through the crowd.

I leapt into his arms and gave him an octopus hug he was clearly unprepared for. Tía Sofia was standing next to him, smiling, short and trim. She seemed delighted to see me, although my energetic and unexpected appearance must have surprised her.

My exuberance almost knocked her over.

Andrés put me down and we greeted each other, sizing one another up with shared affection and curiosity.

He had grown a new sparse beard, and his longish black hair was trained back into an ambitious ponytail. The scarlet and black welt of a healing bruise beneath his bloodshot left eye surprised me.

I was an inch or so taller than I had been the last time he saw me.

For a disturbing split second as we smiled rather foolishly at one another, I sensed how much we'd grown apart and wondered how our relationship may have changed.

His deepened voice and the intensity and confidence he'd gained in so short a time were so striking I wondered if they'd raise a barrier between us.

He was wearing a smart, wide-brimmed black hat of a style I'd never seen before. Two long red feathers with black tips slanted up from the band.

"Where did you get *that*?" I asked.

He took it off and placed it on my head. It was too large and settled over my ears.

"It suits you," he said. "Now you've turned into an Aussie."

"I've turned into a what?"

"An Aussie. An Australian."

"Why?"

"It was given to me by a friend of mine, Tony Pickett. He's an Aboriginal Australian art student. He came here with a sculptor I got to know, Clement Meadmore. We helped him with his sculpture for the Cultural Olympics. They went home the day before yesterday. When I went to see Tony off at the airport, he gave it to me because I'd been admiring it. I'd told him I was part Tarahumaran and he thought I'd appreciate it. Which I do."

He took back the hat and pointed.

"These are the tail feathers of a red-tailed black cockatoo. Tony called it a *Kaarak*, named for its call. It's common where he lives."

"I like it. It looks good on you, but it's not a magic hat. It hasn't turned me into an Aussie. I'm still a Mexican Rarámuri, and so are you. We'll never change."

He smiled as he put it back on.

"No, it's not a magic hat and I'm still me. But it is Australian. They call it an *Akubra*."

"*Akubra?* Is that an Aboriginal word too?"

He gave a burst of laughter and shook his finger under my nose. "Trust you. Yes, it is. Tony told me it means 'something covering your head' in the Gathang language of his Biripi people, if I remember correctly."

"A-ku-bra," I pronounced each syllable of the word aloud and followed it excitedly with, "Ka-a-rak. My first two Australian Aboriginal words."

Holding both their hands, I dragged Andrés and Tía Sofia along the concourse at a trot towards Papá and Tío Guillermo, who were making their way towards us.

An hour later, Tía Sofia served us a selection of tasty *aperitivos y bebidas*, appetisers and drinks.

Andrés and I were standing among the polished green and multicoloured leaves of a jungle of indoor plants and hanging baskets on the balcony of the unit.

We were four stories up.

The open sliding windows overlooked the historical plaza,

Leaning across the window ledge beside Andrés in the clear air so high up, I was fascinated by the excavated Aztec ruins spread out below us.

A flight of steps led down from the paved plaza to several circular and pyramidal platforms. Andrés told me they were the foundations of ancient temples in the market city of Tlatelolco, destroyed by Hernán Cortés and his conquistadors in August, 1521.

"I know all about him," I burst out. "We're doing a special project on him at school."

He pointed out the ancient Spanish Church of Santiago to our left. It was the first one built by Franciscan fathers to replace the Aztec temples destroyed by Cortés, he explained; and the college and convent of Santa Cruz beside it was opened fifteen years later in 1536. It was a school built to educate the Nahuatl-speaking Indian children.

In the background, surrounding the plaza on three sides, were modern buildings many storeys high. The tallest one beyond the church was a skyscraper housing the Foreign Affairs Office.

"The other buildings are all apartments similar to this one." Andrés pointed around the square. "So we have Aztec and Spanish colonial architecture next to a modern housing complex. That's why it's called the Plaza of Three Cultures."

He gave out a whistling sigh.

"You should have seen this area before it was cleared for the Olympics. It was a slum. As far as you could see. A shantytown for railway workers, peasants new to the city and the homeless unemployed. Many indigenous Indian people were among them. Smoke, dust and filth everywhere. Not to mention rats. A place everyone avoided like the plague, which you may have risked catching if you'd visited."

"Where are those people now?"

"Who knows?" he replied, as Papá called him into the lounge. He shrugged his shoulders. "They've moved on, God knows where to. Swept aside and under the carpet, as usual." He paused, then added with thoughtful sarcasm, "Thanks to the Olympics.'

He glanced back at me as he strode away.

"So much for the Mexican miracle and all the promises of the revolution fifty years ago. The poor are still the poor, and the illiterate are still uneducated. By the tens of millions."

I wasn't sure what he meant. I was puzzled by his references to recent history and I was concerned at the frustration in his voice.

I hadn't heard him speak with such bitterness before. Especially his last words as he disappeared inside, "We have a responsibility to care, *mi pequeña cabra montañosa*. To voice our objections and change things for the better."

It was so out of character it made me wonder how much else he'd changed.

Then a reassuring glow ran through me. *He has remembered to call me his little mountain goat.*

3

Moments later, I heard Papá angrily raise his voice.

"I warned you not to get tangled up with the National Strike Committee, Andrés. You're inviting trouble for all of us."

Hearing his sharp and critical tone, I stiffened.

Listening in without looking around, I watched a family of four or five picnicking on a patch of lawn below. One of the older children was redirecting a plump brown baby crawling half-naked towards plates of food laid out on a colourful Huichol blanket. The dreamlike scene was like a sundrenched tapestry beside the ancient excavations as I listened to the argument.

"Only the extremist rebels among us want to interrupt the Olympics." Andrés's raised voice was replying to a question I hadn't heard. "And I'm not one of them."

"So what *are* you looking to achieve with all this nonsense?'

"Simple. We want to negotiate. We want to have an open democratic dialogue with the government, preferably with the president himself, which he denies us."

"An open democratic dialogue with the president? Get real. Don't you know who you're dealing with? He's a dictator who's got two more years of his six-year presidency to do things for Mexico his way. He and his party leaders are deaf to criticism. He's going to take your demonstrations as a personal insult." Papá sighed a long impatient outbreath. "Is there anything else you students want?"

"We want all political prisoners released. They're all common criminals according to him. We want compensation for those who've suffered police brutality and the families of those who've died. And we want to end the violence of the granaderos. In fact, we want them punished and disbanded, and their leaders dismissed."

"You don't want much." Papá's voice was cutting. "You've heard the rumours—Cuban agitators have taken over the student movement. Not to mention the Russian KGB.'

"That's ridiculous. Yes, we have some communists among us, but very few. We aren't a political party looking to overturn the government. We don't want to depose Díaz Ordaz and his ministers. The only change we want is to repeal the laws allowing for any public demonstration to be crushed with a show of force, no matter how peaceful it is."

"I warned you. The president will never concede," Papá shouted "Don't you realise? If it wasn't for the Olympics, he might—*just might*—consider your demands, but it's too late. So you *are* going to cause the Games to be cancelled."

"No, we're not. Not deliberately. But the president *is*, him and his ministers, Echevarría and Barragán, by clamping down on us so brutally."

"Don't shift the blame, Andrés. *Se necesitan dos para bailar un tango*, it takes two to tango. And as for the brutality you mention, if you provoke a cornered snake, what will it do? It will strike and bite. And what's worse, by threatening the Olympics the way you are you're giving Ordaz an open invitation to go to any extreme to shut you down. I dread to think what he'll do next. Open fire on the lot of you?"

After a brief, tense silence, Andrés's voice was surprisingly firm.

"I told you. Now the Games are only ten days away, most of us want them to go ahead successfully as much as everyone else. Take a look around. None of the street signs or decorations have been damaged. There's no graffiti on any of the venues or the sculptures. Hundreds of students are already working as volunteer guides and hostesses for incoming tourists and visitors. We haven't held up the preparations, and we haven't interfered with any of the cultural events. In fact, I've enjoyed attending some of them."

"For example?"

"Well, the art exhibitions, for a start."

He said it with such unexpected enthusiasm I turned around. I leaned back against the balcony with my arms outstretched along the window ledge gazing at him. His expression was calmer than the fury I'd expected. It caught me by surprise.

"Such as?" Papá asked.

"Well, I've seen Paul Gauguin's *Vairumati*, painted in Tahiti for a start. Such colours and brilliant application of the paint. It's so alive, and every brushstroke is visible on rough sackcloth, because he had no canvases. And Salvador Dali's *Cosmic Athlete*. It's fantastic, a discus thrower about to tear the yellow sun from the sky and hurl it across the universe. Surrealist painter René Magritte, his painting *The Memory*. Unforgettable. The white bust of a woman in profile with a bleeding bullet wound at her temple. As if her memories are seeping away. And the music concerts. Samuel Ashkenazi on his violin. Dave Brubeck and Herbie Mann, jazzing up the crowds on the streets, most of them students, like me and my friends."

Papá, his face still flushed, glanced over and surprised me with a grin.

"It sounds as if Andrés here has been broadening his education at last, *mijita*. Mexico will make a gentleman of him yet."

He turned back to Andrés, giving him a reconciling pat on the shoulder.

"What about your studies? How are they going?"

"Good. As well as you can expect. Physical Education is straightforward. I have time for training and an effective coaching routine. And the running's going well."

"You're looking fit… apart from the black eye."

They both laughed.

"I won't ask," Papá said.

"I came off second best with a soldier's fist."

"Did you now. What about your secondary subjects?'

"All of us on the architecture course have been helping Señor Ramírez Vázquez and the sculptors working on the Ruta de la Amistad, the Friendship Route."

"We saw one of the sculptures when we were landing," I said excitedly from across the room. "Ursa Major. I loved it."

"Yes. The one beside the Sports Palace. It's called *The Big Dipper*. I like it, too," Andrés replied.

"Which ones did you work on?" Papá asked.

'Just the one. I helped the Australian, Clement Meadmore, with his sculpture—*Janus*. We put the steel rods and mesh framework in place and helped with the concrete pour. It looks simple now, but it was complicated. It took us months.'

He pointed at the Akubra he'd hung behind the door.

"One of his Australian students gave that to me when he flew out."

"Janus, what does it look like?" I asked, as I walked across the lounge.

"Imagine a long cube twisted up into a ring like an open Möbius strip, six metres high and the same across. Its square ends face in opposite directions. Then try pouring blackened concrete into it." He grinned. "That's what we did. With difficulty. Meadmore had a great sense of humour. Beers all around when we succeeded. VB was the brand, I remember, because he was from Melbourne, he told us. Specially imported for the occasion. I had to write the project up as an assignment. I scored an A. I'll show it to you later. You can see the sculpture itself tomorrow, if you like. It's simple but impressive."

"I like," I said. "Show us the whole city. Especially the Olympic stadium."

"Of course. I can miss tomorrow's marches. They're all going to end up right here, in any case, at a meeting on the Tlatelolco Plaza below. The Strike Committee members want to talk to us. I've heard a rumour they may be calling for a temporary truce."

Tía Sofia appeared in the hallway and beckoned me to the bedroom she'd allocated to Papá and me. Without a word, she pointed at two new dresses she'd laid out side by side on my camp bed.

The first was a smart white blouse and mini-skirt combination with the Mexico 1968 logo imprinted on it in dazzling black op art, a labyrinth of wavy lines based on Huichol Indian designs. It was identical to those I'd seen several Olympic hostesses wearing at the airport, though theirs had been pastel orange. It had a cloak attached to the back of the collar.

The second was a white trapeze dress with aquamarine figures running across it.

"That's the uniform of the hostesses at the athletics," she said, pointing at the second. "I thought you'd like it. Aquamarine for track and field. Each sport has a special colour."

"I love them both," I said as I hugged her. "*Muchas gracias, Tía Sofia. Muchísimas gracias.* Thank you, thank you. Can I try them on?"

"Go ahead. A full-length mirror is in my room, through there." She pointed at the door on her right. "We'll wait for you in the lounge."

They both fitted, with a little room to spare.

When I reappeared in front of everyone in the lounge I stole the show.

I paraded along an imaginary catwalk and back, spinning to show the swirl of the trapeze skirt and balancing next on tiptoe in the miniskirt as if I was wearing stiletto heels.

Tía Sofia announced for me.

One minute I was a leading model for Courrèges at the Paris Fashion Week according to her, and the next a model for Mary Quant in Carnaby Street—even though I'd never heard of either fashion house.

For several electrifying, unforgettable minutes, the applause and laughter were intoxicating.

I acknowledged my admirers and accepted a bouquet from Andrés—a bunch of fresh carnations, reds, whites, yellows and pinks. He withdrew them from a large crystal vase shaped like an Olympic torch on the coffee table. Their long stems were dripping water in translucent pearls. I caught some in my palm and gleefully splashed them over him kneeling in front of me, before I returned the flowers to the vase once the show was over.

The only person missing from the audience is Mamá. I wondered. *Or is she here with us?*

5

After breakfast the next morning, Papá was the first to leave the table. He was going to work on the Mining Industry exhibit.

"I'll see you all tomorrow," he said. "I'll be working late, so I'll book in to UNAM tonight."

He ruffled my hair before I could stop him and blew me a kiss.

"You enjoy yourself, *mijita*, and don't give Tío Guillermo or Tía Sofia too much trouble."

He gave Andrés an amused look, shaking a forefinger, his eyebrows raised.

"And you, *mi joven rebelde con una causa*, my young rebel with a cause, take good care of her… and don't even think of enrolling her in one of your female student brigades we see on the news all the time."

"Why not?" I asked cheekily. "I might enrol myself—"

"No, you won't. *Todo eso de tirar sosténes*, throwing away and burning their bras! They're scandalous."

"Scandalous? They're brilliant," Andrés said, reaching for another slice of pan dulce while he still had a mouthful. "Even someone as old as you must have heard of *liberación femenina*, women's liberation?"

"Anyway, I don't wear a bra yet," I pointed out.

Papá clicked his tongue and shook his finger at me. "That doesn't qualify you to join."

He turned and raised his open palm. "Enjoy yourselves."

He bent to pick up his briefcase and strode to the door, closing it behind him. We heard him clattering down the steps to the lift.

Tío Guillermo remained with us.

He had agreed to take the day off and drive me and Andrés around the city to see the Olympic decorations, the sculptures and the sporting venues.

"We'll start with the Sports' Palace and *The Big Dipper*," he said, nodding at me in the mirror with a confidential wink as we took the crowded lift to the ground floor.

I returned it with a shy and awkward grin. I was self-conscious and unsure around him. I felt so small and insignificant beside his overpowering presence, especially in such a confined space, even though I'd known him all my life.

"You've seen it from the air, so you know what to expect. And it's the closest. Just a few kilometres southeast of here. Then we'll drive across the city and see the sights."

As soon as we turned into the traffic streaming along Paseo de la Reforma Avenue and headed south, I relaxed and was enchanted.

The city came vibrantly alive, the way I remembered it when Papá and I had come down to watch Andrés run in the cross country.

White-painted tree trunks glided across the front of shops freshly painted in brilliant pastel colours as we passed, gaudy rectangular billboards advertising the Olympics erected over their open doorways.

And *there*, on the left, the brilliant mural portrait of a man and a woman standing side by side I remembered, three storeys high, completely covering the facades of two neighbouring flat-roofed buildings.

Occasional autumn leaves cascading from the liquidambar trees skittered across the car's bonnet. They fluttered away in the slipstream.

One became trapped and rattled in the windscreen wiper, so Andrés leaned half his body dangerously out to clear it. He whooped to the music on the radio and surprised passers-by who looked around to watch his double-jointed gymnastics.

A huge bronze monument loomed up on the left. It was dedicated to the Aztec leaders Cuitláhuac and Cuauhtemoc. It showed a gigantic warrior in full war dress, his spear raised threateningly against the sky. I read the names embedded in the pyramidal platform as we passed.

"Do either of you know anything about them?" Tío Guillermo asked, jerking a thumb at the statue as he turned eastwards around it.

"The battle of *Noche Triste*," I called out from the back seat. "The battle of the Night of Sorrow. We've just finished a project on Hernán Cortés at school. Cuitláhuac and his warriors killed so many of his conquistadors that Cortés had to retreat from Tenochtitlán." I struggled to remember. "From Tlatelolco too, I think. On 30 June, 1520, wasn't it?"

"Yes, you're right. From Tlatelolco as well," Tío Guillermo said. "It took Cortés over a year to rally his troops and retake Tenochtitlán."

"Helped by the Tlaxcalan Indian tribes," I said. "They hated the Aztecs."

"And his African slaves. He had hundreds of them with him. I knew you'd know," Tío said.

He knew I'd know? Is he complimenting me? Or is it an ironic observation and he's being sarcastic?

"Cuitláhuac's spirit is alive and well," Andrés remarked drily. "He lives on in Alicia's DNA."

"Yours too," I said.

"Not tonight, I hope," Tío Guillermo replied. "Tonight, he and his warriors can leave us in peace to enjoy Tía Sofia's cooking. Don't you agree?"

"As long as we can call on him if we need backup against the granaderos." Andrés laughed. "And whatever Tía Sofia cooks, it'll have to be good to beat the Polytechnic Zacatenco campus canteen. It's five-star, believe it or not."

"I guarantee you'll score hers a six, if not seven stars. How do fish enchiladas for afternoon comida sound?"

"What type of fish?"

"Tilapia, homegrown. A friend of a friend runs an aquaculture farm just outside Buenavista. They jump straight from the ponds into the pan."

"There it is," I yelled, as the giant armadillo I'd seen from the air swept into view.

6

We spent the next half hour walking around the Sports Palace among other groups. I thought most of them must be recently arrived tourists or athletes visiting the city.

The basketball stadium was closed to visitors, but we admired the complicated design and shining roof from the outside. The concrete paving around it was decorated in bright blue and orange concentric semi-circles.

Beside it, the seven concrete pillars of *The Big Dipper* stood dwarfing us.

I lay on my back to take a second photograph of them to match the one I took from the plane. From that angle, the gleaming copper dome with its spikes was sharply etched against the bluest sky, across which windswept sunlit clouds spread in dizzying brushstrokes.

As I was kneeling to put the camera back in the case, Andrés nudged me with his foot.

He nodded at two men strolling past.

One of them glanced briefly at me in my hostess's uniform as I fiddled with the camera.

"Plainclothes security police," Andrés hissed as they walked on.

I felt a quiver of fear run up and down my back.

When they were a reasonable distance away he spoke aloud, his voice sarcastic. "They're officers of the *Batallón Olimpia*, the Olympic Battalion. I'd recognize them anywhere. Keeping us all safe and sound. They're everywhere you look."

I glanced around and picked out several other groups of men similarly dressed in casual clothes, strolling among the crowd in twos and threes. I'd earlier taken them for visitors.

"Don't let them worry you," he said, as we walked on.

"I'm not worried."

I tried to sound convincing as I slung the camera over my shoulder and caught up with him.

"Oh, sure. You don't look it. Ignore them. Relax."

Back in the car, we crossed the city.

I was fascinated by the graphic beauty of the Olympic signs and the venue icons,

There were transparent plastic banners imprinted with white doves and multi-coloured half-moons strung across the streets and the buildings.

There were balloons everywhere in eye-catching colours and various sizes and colourful two-metre-high hexagonal information pillboxes on the pavements. They carried directions to the sports venues on all sides.

I especially liked the rooftop billboards telegraphing the message "*Todo es posible en paz*", "Everything is possible in peace", written in Spanish, English, French, Arabic and Chinese.

The buses I saw were smartly painted with the psychedelic Mexico 1968 logo and most of the passing cars had showy bumper stickers on them.

Even the lamp posts, I noticed, were painted in unique colours for each street—I saw pink on Churubusco Avenue leading away from the Sports Palace, green along the Río de la Piedad we followed across the city, and orange on the Periférico Sur Ring Road we were then driving down.

"They're blue all the way to Xochimilco," Tío Guillermo said over his shoulder when I commented on them. "You can follow them to the different venues. Each has its distinct colour. The committee even wanted to paint the pavements, but never got round to it."

I was so excited I wanted to tell Tío how the overall effect of the decorations and signs so joyfully communicated Mexico's electric atmosphere it took my breath away, but I felt sheepish and the words I was looking for escaped me.

"It's wonderful, Tío. Truly wonderful. I'll never forget it," was the best I could come up with.

Andrés turned and nodded at me. 'You're impressed, hey? You just wait. We have more surprises up ahead. The sculptures on the Friendship Route. Eighteen concrete ones, to be exact, and another four in bronze and steel. Are you ready?'

"We won't have time to stop at all of them," Tío Guillermo said.

He lifted his thick-boned left wrist and displayed the dial of his gold watch embedded on a mat of wiry black hair. It showed eleven-thirty.

"We can stop for one or two you might want to photograph—and slow down for the rest. You choose the ones you really like."

I hesitated, and then asked, "How can I decide until I've seen them all, Tío? I need to compare them first, before I choose."

Andrés gave a burst of laughter.

"Still pedantic as ever, *mi pequeña quisquillosa*, my little nitpicker. Will you ever change?" He leaned across the seat and stared back at me. "You're going to make a brilliant lawyer."

"Linguist, you mean."

"*Oooh* yes. How could I forget? Our up-and-coming translator, our walking dictionary. Our own *La Malinche*, speaking in tongues—just like she did for Hernán Cortés." He looked across to the right. "Okay. Here comes the first sculpture. What do you think?"

I stared at the two towering sculptures, unsure what they represented.

"They look like a pair of bull's horns," I said. "One black, one white… or hockey sticks for giants."

"We'd better not let the sculptor know." Andrés laughed again. "She might take you seriously and use you for a hockey ball. She's called it *Signals*. What about the next one? See it over there through the trees?"

"Ah, that one I don't mind.'

I liked the way the vivid blue-green circular pieces slotted together like a jigsaw. Andrés said it was called *The Anchor*, constructed by a Swiss sculptor he'd met.

"It's nice," I said, looking back.

I took the camera out and asked Tío Guillermo to slow down for the next one. I focussed and snapped the three monumental columns as we passed. They reminded me of those making up *The Big Dipper*, but their brilliant colour was a beautiful shade of purple I had never seen before.

"What colour's that?" I asked.

"Red violet, I'd say," Tío Guillermo replied. "Almost magenta. I don't know if there's a special name for it… *plum*, perhaps?"

"That was *The Three Graces*," Andrés said. "By Miloslav someone or other, from Czechoslovakia, as far as I remember."

"Easily the best so far."

And so it went, as we drove past another nine.

Then we drew into the parking lot of the Athletes' Village. We stopped to buy a grilled corn *elote* each, covered in tasty melted *cotija* cheese and sprinkled with ground chilli and lime juice.

Andrés took a photo of me eating mine sitting side-saddle on a three-metre-high maroon metal sculpture of the Mexico 1968 logo in the plaza. I climbed it using the Olympic rings for footholds.

Back in the car, we turned up Insurgentes Sur Avenue and followed the aqua lamp posts to the Olympic stadium.

I was speechless at the gigantic sweep of its dimensions.

We joined a tour group and were shown into an upper tier in the stadium. We had a clear view of the immaculate red tartan track, the immense expanse of lawn marked up for the field events, the water jump for the steeplechase, and halfway along the back straight, the ninety-three steps leading up the pyramid to the cauldron, which I had run up during the trials.

"I can't believe we watched you run right here," I said to Andrés. "You must have been jumping out of your skin."

"I was impressed," he admitted. "At first, that is. But once the pistol fired…"

"I can't *wait* for the opening ceremony. And for the fifteenth and sixteenth, when we'll be sitting here watching."

"Me too. They can't come soon enough," Andrés replied. "I'm glad the black Americans from the United States have decided to come. They were talking about going on strike to protest for their civil rights under the Black Power movement. The Games would have been a disappointment without them. Especially the sprinters."

"What are civil rights?" I asked.

"Making certain everyone enjoys the same opportunities in society, no matter what your race or religion is."

"Don't they have that in the United States?'

"No, it's complicated. In some states, the blacks are separated from the whites. By law. It's called segregation—now there's another interesting word for you. In the buses. In the cafés. Even in the schools and universities." He looked down at me with sudden seriousness. "Don't worry about it. It's a long story, and anyway, they're coming to compete, so we will see them."

"Good." I held up the camera. "I'll make sure I take this."

"You'd better. I'm looking forward to watching the Africans in the distance events. A few of them have been training in the IPN grounds and I've joined them doing speed work once or twice. They're brilliant runners, from Kenya. They're so… I don't know, so relaxed. So natural. So *streamlined*."

"As if they've been running all their lives, like us?"

"Exactly. And they're friendly. Always laughing."

"What languages do they speak?"

"They're from East Africa, so they must speak Swahili among themselves, I guess. Or tribal languages, like us."

I looked up at him. "Can you find out for me, please?"

His gaze met mine and he nodded, his eyes carrying the hint of a sardonic smile.

"Did you talk to any of them?"

"One, to start with—Kimaru Songok. He's a four-hundred-metre hurdler. He spoke to me in English, so we understood each other, more or less. He introduced me to some of the distance runners. Kip was one I remember. Wilson. And Amos. I forget the others. Oh yes, and Naftali, how could I forget him? We ran some laps together and I enjoyed it."

He smiled.

"They don't just have four on the floor. They have overdrive and rocket power in reserve. It's going to be interesting. They asked me about Juan Martínez, and when I warned them he was a front runner with stamina to burn, Kimaru told me that's exactly what they were looking for."

When we returned to the Periférico Sur Ring Road, Andrés said, "We've saved the best two sculptures for last, and there they are, over on the left."

We stopped at both.

The first was Australian Clement Meadmore's *Janus*, just as Andrés had described it—a solid black cube twisted into an upright ring six metres tall. Its ends faced in opposite directions parallel to the ground.

We climbed the steps carved into the volcanic rock on which it was placed so that I could shoot it close-up.

I liked the simplicity and flow "Why is it called *Janus?*" I asked.

"Janus was a Roman God with two faces, front and back. He could look both ways at once. See the ends up there, facing east and west?" Andrés replied. "He was the God of doorways. The God of beginnings and endings. He could see into the future and the past simultaneously. *Es pore so que Enero se lleva su nombre*, that's why January's named after him."

"But why is it black?"

"I asked Tony Pickett the same question. He told me Meadmore had dedicated the sculpture to an Aboriginal hero of his."

He bent and pointed out a name and the date 1894 carved into concrete at the base.

"Jandamarra," I read aloud as I focussed the camera and photographed it.

"Tony told me Jandamarra fought a war against the invading British colonists in Western Australia, just like Cuitláhuac when he defeated Hernán Cortés."

He waited for a moment as I took in what he'd said, before going on.

"He saw the terrible future unfolding for his people when the colonists arrived. He fought to save his tribe from the annihilation he saw coming."

Then we drove on to the last sculpture a short distance away.

"Now *this* one takes the prize," I said as we parked, and I jumped out.

"It's called *Articulated Wall*," Andrés said as we left the car.

I focussed the Leica.

"It's also Señor Ramírez Vázquez's favourite," Andrés said, "but I'd say it comes a close second to *Janus*. What do you say, Tío Guillermo?"

"Oh no. No, no, no. You two can fight it out. I never get involved in family matters when blood's about to be spilled." He gave me a shrewd, amused look and placed his hand on my shoulder. "I know what this little cat's like when she's got her claws out."

I walked around the sculpture, taking several photos, before stepping back to admire it.

It was seventeen metres tall and painted a brilliant yellow.

I counted thirty-three identically sized rectangular slabs of reinforced concrete, one above the other.

I read their dimensions on the information placard.

Each one was twelve metres long, one and a half metres wide and half a metre thick. They were mounted on an invisible central steel axis with a tiny but visible gap between them. Each block was placed slightly askew from those above and below it.

In three sets of eight, their edges curved out and back to create a wave-like effect up the column, with five at the base and four at the top, complementing the spiral.

It was brilliantly designed, the play of light and shadow across it captivating.

"Ten out of ten!" I yelled, sprinting around it. 'Without a doubt. Maybe even eleven!"

"That settles the matter, and no blood spilled." Tío Guillermo said, laughing as Andrés caught up with me and attacked my ticklish ribs, as always, with the bony fingers of his left hand. "Time to head for home and enjoy the tilapia."

We turned off Insurgentes Sur Avenue, intending to take a shortcut through the back streets, but we were held up behind a long column of army trucks filled with soldiers.

"Probably the paratroopers," Andrés informed me. "They're in the city all the time these days."

"But they're all armed," I said.

"They always are. They've been attending our demonstrations lately to give the granaderos backup and make sure we keep the peace. We're used to it."

When Tío Guillermo turned onto a parallel street to overtake them, I was astonished at the time it took, truck after truck still visible on the adjoining side street as we passed.

When we passed the front of the column, there were five rubber-tyred armoured vehicles leading them, like those I'd seen on TV in the last few months, driving through the scattering demonstrators to disperse them.

I suddenly felt sick and my stomach churned at the memory. I fought to prevent myself from throwing up.

"Tío! I'm feeling car sick," I shouted, desperately swallowing the saliva pouring into my mouth.

Tío Guillermo pulled up, allowing me to open the door and sit with my head between my knees in the fresh air until the nausea passed.

When we pulled into the Chihuahua building car park at last, I raced to the lift lobby, sheepish with relief and embarrassed by my reaction.

I took the steps at a light jog to regain my composure.

They'd arrived in the lift just before me and the front door to the flat was open when I reached the corridor.

I hugged Tía Sofia when she offered me her motherly concern, before moving to the balcony, sliding open the windows and leaning out to look down.

There were small groups already gathering on the plaza beside the church to attend the political meeting Andrés had mentioned.

Others were arriving through the entrances to the laneway on the left and right. Many were carrying red carnations in bunches and single flowers. Others had them in a buttonhole or visible in a shirt pocket.

Andrés had told us earlier it was an emblem the students had adopted.

A *pajarero*, a seller of songbirds, stood out among them.

He was so unexpected I changed the film and snapped him making his way across the paving. The tower of bamboo cages strapped to his back swayed with every stride. Each cage was decorated with red and yellow crepe paper hibiscus flowers and filled with shadowy, fluttering pairs of dark blue songbirds and orange-chested green parakeets.

The church bell sounded three o'clock when Tía Sofia served the tilapia enchiladas for a late *comida*. Aromatic smells poured from the kitchen the moment she opened the oven door. They enriched the lighter hints of spice and garlic lingering before then.

"Can we go down and join the students on the plaza now?" I asked when we'd finished.

Tío Guillermo looked at me, carefully refolding his serviette. "It's not a good idea. Not after the way you were feeling just an hour ago."

"I'm fine."

I widened my eyes, giving him my special pleading look. It always worked with Papá.

"There's nothing wrong with me now."

"You're too young, Alicia. It could get rough down there."

"There are other kids my age in the crowd, even younger. I even saw a pregnant lady pushing a pram, with two little ones following her."

"Even so, you've had a long day."

"Please?"

"You heard me."

His patience is running out. Perhaps just one more.

"Please?"

He pursed his lips. "Are you going down, Andrés?" he asked, his tone irritated.

Elated, but not showing it, I knew I was winning him around.

"No, I'm not planning to. It's my day off training and I'm looking forward to an early night." Andrés turned and bowed to Tía Sofia. "Especially after the best enchilada I've ever tasted. Seven stars, Tío? Ten, in my book."

"Please, please, please. Just for a little while. I want to feel what it's like to mix with students and school kids, even school kids my age, getting together to speak up for a just cause."

Tío Guillermo leaned back and looked at Andrés again, drumming his fingers on the table.

It wasn't much, but it was enough.

I gazed directly at him, mustering my most beguiling smile. "Pleeeease?"

"Alright," he said at last, glancing at his watch. "You rest up here until five-thirty, and we'll go down for an hour. No longer. When I say so, we come straight back upstairs. No ifs, no buts."

"Gracias! Gracias, Tío!" I squealed, surprising myself by running around the table to hug him. "I can take the Leica with me and get some more shots."

Now all I had to do was convince Andrés to join us. I knew he was enjoying a rest day between training sessions. I didn't say a word, just looked at him with as pleading an expression as I could muster.

"No, it's my day off—and *nothing* comes between me and my running," Andrés said when he saw my look. "Nothing. You above all people know that."

"*Please,* please, please, please… I want to finish the film in the camera," I begged him.

"Alright, I'll come," he surprised me by changing his mind. "I wouldn't do it for anyone else. Only for you, to take your photos." He gave me a quick dry laugh, his voice touched with sarcasm. "You never know, your photos might go down in history, *pequeña cabra.*"

"Like Abu Xavier's Guernica," I agreed excitedly, ignoring his tone, and triumphant at convincing him to come.

10

We took the lift down to the plaza and it was packed, people streaming in through both entrances. Tío Guillermo showed his displeasure with an exasperated shake of his head as we exchanged looks and joined the flow.

"We're not going to enjoy this." He gave me a thin smile. "There must be ten or fifteen thousand people here already."

I held up the camera and snapped his expression just as I was jostled sideways.

"At least let me use up this film, Tío. I've just changed it. I've already taken two—one of you and one of the *pajarero* over there. There are twenty-two exposures left."

"*Only* twenty-two? As long as you make it quick."

He frowned down at the red carnation he was carrying. Andrés had removed one for each of us from the vase. I saw Tío notice some people around him were not carrying one, so he threaded it through a buckle on the camera case slung around my shoulder.

Tía Sofia had snipped the stem off mine and pinned it to my top pocket.

Beside me, Andrés acknowledged two smiling dark-haired girls his age in the passing crowd. He threw the nearest one his carnation. She caught it, giving him an approving look before they both turned jauntily away. I snapped them too late, capturing the girl with the carnation waving Andrés goodbye with it over her shoulder. They disappeared towards the church, where someone was talking through loudspeakers.

"That's Gloria," he said, "and the other one's Ana María. They're in my architecture class. Gloria worked with us on *Janus*."

"She likes you."

"Who doesn't?" he responded at once, with a teasing self-effacing expression, leaving me unsure whether he was joking or serious.

I took him at his word and dug my elbow into his ribs. "Me, for one, when you're boasting."

We worked our way to the back edge of the crowd close to the church, the voice on the speakers clearer now. A group of schoolboys in maroon and khaki uniforms in front of me restricted my view. One of them, whose features I recognised as Tepehuán Indian, flashed me a brief smile and stepped to one side when he saw my dilemma. The blond student next to him was pushed to the left.

When I raised both arms above my head to take a hopeful random shot, Tío Guillermo took me by the armpits and effortlessly lifted me to his broad shoulders without so much as asking.

I almost dropped the camera, but the position was perfect.

I had a bird's eye view across the plaza and was able to balance my elbows on his bald head. He was rock solid each time I said I was about to take another shot.

I ranged the camera across the crowd and took several shots in quick succession.

The first was the pregnant lady with the black pram, standing stock-still and listening intently. Her two little kids—*are they twin girls?*—were squatting on the paving beside her, playing what looked like cat's cradle with a web of black string. I was delighted when the nearest of them stuck out her tongue when she saw the camera.

Another was a broad view of the Chihuahua building. A central balcony window on the third floor was wide open, a border of white sheets drawing attention to it. There was a pair of black loudspeakers at each end of the window ledge in the hallway beside the lift shaft. There were several figures in the window, one of them speaking into a microphone.

"The Strike Committee," Andrés said as I took the shots. "Just as I thought. They want to call the demonstration off.

They're concerned about the number of *granaderos* and riot police already here."

"Clearly, they know something we don't," Tío Guillermo agreed.

The reaction from some rowdy groups in the crowd to their announcement shocked me. They began shouting in unison, others joining them, *"No queremos Olimpiadas, queremos revolución.* We don't want the Olympics; we want a revolution."

The chant became deafening, drowning out whatever warning the student was broadcasting down at us.

"Malditos extremistos, bloody extremists," Andrés yelled at us. "I should have known they'd be here."

I was surprised to see a single line of helmeted soldiers placed an arm's length apart at the base of the Chihuahua building, facing the crowd. They were standing at ease beneath the concrete overhang, bayonets fixed, as though guarding the entrances to the stairwells and the line of shop front windows. An officer stood at the centre. His uniform was immaculate and his polished epaulettes shone. He was holding a large orange megaphone in his right hand.

"It's the presidential guard, by the look of the uniforms," Andrés said.

I photographed the officer, before raising the camera to focus on two helicopters that appeared out of the growing dusk high above us. One was painted in dark blue police colours, the other in army grey camouflage.

The crowd quietened as they circled for several minutes. They seemed to be observing us, until two brilliant red flares were fired from the top floor of the Foreign Affairs skyscraper to our right.

I took a dramatic shot of the flares falling against the darkening sky, trailing what looked like flames. They exploded on the paving between the church and the Chihuahua building, people beneath the line of their descent screaming as they fought to escape the shower of sparks.

The church bell unexpectedly rang out, tolling six and silencing the crowd.

People close to me looked up at the bell tower, some laughing, others clearly counting out the chimes.

I held my breath, the eeriness of the moment made me suspect it was a warning signal.

For several minutes the student's voice crackling over the loudspeakers urged the crowd to disperse, before falling silent as the police helicopter swooped directly at us. Tension rippled through the crowd as it also fired two flares aimed at the plaza, this time one red, one green. They had same incendiary descent and explosive result.

The crowd scattered as they struck the ground.

The helicopter skimmed low across the buildings, before soaring up and hovering over us, alongside the army helicopter once again.

The stunned silence lengthened. It was broken by the: *Whup! Whup! Whup!* of helicopter blades.

Then a group of helmeted soldiers carrying rifles with bayonets fixed burst from behind the church wall to our right. They charged forward and took up positions in front of the church, facing the crowd. In a strange, dreamlike sequence, a side door of the church opened, and I photographed a number of men in plain clothes pouring down the steps, the door slamming shut behind them. The first of them showed a sheet of paper to the surrounding soldiers, who let them through.

Wearing white gloves on one hand and carrying black pistols in the other, they melted purposefully into the crowd.

One of them passed so close to Andrés he could have reached out and touched him.

Andrés looked up at me. "The Olympic Battalion! And they're armed. It means trouble."

As he spoke, I heard the sharp crack of a gunshot, followed by several others.

I ducked when I heard their terrifying echoes.

Then I raised the camera again, fighting to control my shaking hands, to capture a soldier in the line beneath the eaves of the Chihuahua building, who had slumped to his knees and toppled forward at the feet of the others.

The officer raised his megaphone and spoke into it, his voice screeching until he adjusted the instrument and yelled at the crowd to leave at once. When he repeated the order, there was another sharp sequence of gunshots coming either from the roof of the church above us or from an upper floor of the Foreign Affairs skyscraper beyond it.

The officer was flung backwards against a shopfront window, hurling aside the megaphone. He slid down the glass, a smear of red marking his descent. He sat on the paving rocking himself, his legs outstretched, clutching at his chest, his mouth wide open coughing gouts of blood across his uniform.

In a shocking otherworldly moment, I read the name of the shop above his head in bold black print—*Fotos Exprés*.

I rushed to take the shot as Tío Guillermo lifted me down.

He took hold of my hand, and we turned to run for the lift well at the far end of the building. The panicked crowd surrounding us rushed with one mind towards the same exit, their screams and shouts incoherent, trampling over those who'd fallen, papers flying as they threw aside the pamphlets and leaflets distributed among them earlier. An older man tore off his white shirt red with blood and waved it overhead in surrender. He staggered across our path before Tío brushed him aside. Others were scrambling for cover behind the vehicles in the car park and crawling beneath them.

When I looked around for Andrés, he wasn't with us.

I screamed a warning at Tío Guillermo.

We slowed and he leaned down to shout in my ear, "He must be ahead of us. Did you see him go?"

Seized with a terrifying degree of dread I screamed at the top of my lungs, "No. He must be back there."

We fought our way back through the chaos of running and falling bodies, kicking aside an overturned black pram, slipping on abandoned shoes and sandals, a handbag, paper cups, a scattering of empty food cartons.

We found Andrés lying face down beside the outstretched body of the blond-haired teenage schoolboy who'd been standing in front of me moments before beside the Tepehuán Indian. A bullet had smashed through the base of the schoolboy's skull and blood was seeping from beneath his body, spreading across the slate tiles on each side of him like a pair of wings with red and black-tipped feathers.

Andrés was groaning, his left calf bleeding into his jeans, shredded where a bullet had torn through them. Tío Guillermo turned him over. There was a grazed lump beneath his hairline and a cut across his nose where he'd struck the tiles.

His eyes were glazed and unfocused.

As I looked down at him the world swirled around me, leaving me frozen with shock. For a moment I had no idea where I was. I doubled over and heard myself scream as though I was someone else, before I heard Tío's voice calling for the camera case. Barely comprehending, I handed it to him. He unclipped the strap, tore off the carnation and bound Andrés's leg above the knee.

Below the wound, his left foot stuck out at a grotesque angle.

Tío stood, took me by my upper arms and shook me, before taking my face in both his hands.

He leaned down to look into my eyes with unforgettable intensity. "Listen, cariño. We have no time. You have to get away from here. Run. Run as fast as you can. I will take Andrés to the Green Cross Hospital. *To the Green Cross Hospital.* Remember that. Now Go. *Go!*"

He turned me around and pushed me away so violently I almost fell.

I regained my footing and stooped to pick up the camera. I stood unmoving in another moment of indecision, watching Tío use his teeth to tighten the knot on a white handkerchief he wrapped around his left hand before lifting Andrés across his back and right shoulder. He manoeuvred Andrés's arms around his neck and gripped both his hands in his right.

"Go!" he shouted again, leaning forward and balancing Andrés on his hip, his trailing legs off the ground. He took his first lunging step towards the exit, his left hand a cloth-bound white fist, raised for balance. "Go! Run like you've never run before."

Helpless, I could not budge.

The world spun around me, my terror-stricken mind a void. I lost all sense of time as a formation of soldiers advanced like black spectres across the plaza. Screaming people were trapped by armoured vehicles and soldiers at the exit to my left.

Some soldiers were firing from the shoulder, some kneeling before advancing again and others sliding into prone positions, one or two with their rifles balanced on the bodies of the fallen.

Closer, in stark black outline, the pregnant woman was crawling away from her pram. She was pinned as if paralysed in the blazing beam of a spotlight directed at the plaza from the police helicopter.

Is she searching for her children among the wounded? Did they try to run? Were they trampled in the stampede? And the horrifying question struck me: *Will the spotlight focus next on me?*

I tore my gaze away and my mind cleared as though I'd received an electric shock.

I had seven exposures left.

I levered rapidly through them on automatic focus to the end of the film, before packing the camera back in the case and snapping it shut.

Then I sprinted along the parapet beside the Aztec excavations, reached a flight of steps leading down into them and leapt down it, three steps at a time.

When I ran along the pathway between the pyramids, the lights in the Chihuahua building were switched off as if someone had cut the power supply. I looked back up to see rapid flashes of gunfire from several open windows on the second and third floors to the right flaring against the pitch-black backdrop, as though someone in there was striking matches.

Less than a hundred metres ahead of me another line of soldiers was advancing towards me in formation, bayonets glinting. They were detaining some people, herding them at bayonet point to the corner where the steel paling fences met. They corralled them there. They were allowing others through. Women and girls, I noticed.

As I passed one of the pyramidal platforms, I climbed partway up and concealed the camera in a crevice between the rocks in its foundations.

I joined two women rushing in silence towards the exit gate. They were dragging a small girl between them and, I could not believe it, a brown silky terrier was straining ahead on a leash, as if they were a family out for a brisk afternoon walk.

When we reached the advancing soldiers they scrutinised us, parted and directed us through. Others on guard at the exit gate inspected us, grinning at my hostess's uniform and confiscating a woven decorated Huichol basket one of the women was carrying before ushering us on.

We did not speak as we walked down Central Lázaro Cárdenas Avenue beneath the trees, a long line of empty army trucks parked beside the pavement.

A short way along we passed several soldiers eating tortillas handed out by someone in the back of a truck. They'd stacked their rifles against the side of the vehicle. They took no notice of us as we passed, seemingly oblivious to the uproar and the sharp crackle of gunfire on the plaza.

A light rain began to fall when we passed the last truck.

I separated from my rescuers, took shelter beneath the awning of an empty takeaway restaurant and sat at one of the tables. I struggled to assure myself I had escaped. The cordon of soldiers had allowed me through. I had not been detained at the gate.

Shaking uncontrollably, I realised I was safe.

I gasped for breath and sobbed when the rain strengthened in a series of wind gusts, drumming on the canvas overhead. It ran down in a blinding sheet before swirling across the pavement towards the gutter.

Just as it was across the plaza, I imagined, *turning a deeper red as it washed away the blood, including Andrés's.*

The full horror of his shooting flooded through me.

My beloved brother Andrés, who's been shot because I convinced him to come to down to the plaza. My heart faltered painfully as I felt an overpowering sense of guilt. *I've ruined Andrés's life. And the metallic smell in the air before I turned to run—what was that? The smell of gunfire or his blood?*

One of the women I'd been walking with burst through a curtain of water.

She shook it from her hair, sat beside me and put her arm around my shoulder. When she asked where I was going and she didn't represent a threat, I told her everything.

Who I was.

That Papá was at work.

That I was living in the Chihuahua building and couldn't
return.

That the last time I'd seen them, my tío had been on the
plaza carrying my brother Andrés to safety—he had been
shot in the leg.

That I had to make my way to the Green Cross Hospital
to meet them.

"You mean the Dr Rubén Leñero Hospital," she said, as
I wept in her arms. "I am Ava. The other lady is my sister,
Carmen. *Ven con nosotras*, come with us. We live just around
the corner next to the Francisco Medina Ascencio Primary
School. We are teachers there. *Te llevaré al hospital mañana*,
I will take you to the hospital tomorrow."

Lighting the Flame, Mexico City 1968 – Courtesy Smith Archives / Alamy stock photo

CHAPTER NINE

1

SEÑORA AVA ARRANGED A straw-filled mattress and bedding on the floor of a storeroom for me.

Shelves lining the walls were crammed with books and files.

The smell was musty. It made me cough at first, and I imagined all the cockroaches that must have been there. I thrashed from side to side in the darkness for what seemed hours, panting, before I fell into a fitful sleep.

When I woke it was still dark.

I lay half-conscious, uncertain where I was. I stared at a wedge of electric light streaming across the unfamiliar ceiling through the partly open door. It threw shadows from the peeling paint in barbed and jagged patterns so terrifying I screamed in sudden panic for Tía Ariché.

When Señora Ava appeared at the door, I rushed sobbing into her open arms.

She led me to her bedroom, where I curled up beside her in the warm bed, trembling. I tried to calm myself, staring across her shoulder at the green flower-patterned curtains lightening with the dawn.

When she fell asleep and began to rhythmically snore, I shut my eyes against nightmarish images arising from the night before, dreading what waited for me in the morning.

After breakfast, Señora Ava drove me to the hospital. The traffic and pedestrians were so chaotic we had to park a street away.

At the hospital, a line of ambulances with green crosses on the side and others with red, as well as private cars, were banked up in the emergency driveway.

Nurses and paramedics were unloading wounded patients onto grey-blanketed gurneys scattered in a triage area on the lawns. They were lifting others from wheelchairs and stretchers back into their vehicles to relocate them elsewhere.

A group of white-and-blue-coated doctors worked purposefully among them.

When we reached the front of the queue, two armed soldiers barred our way.

"If you're bringing in someone wounded," one of them told Señora Ava, "or you need attention yourselves, report at the triage area over there. Otherwise, you must leave. No visitors are allowed this morning. The hospital is out of bounds."

"We're looking for Alicia's brother." Señora Ava placed an open palm behind my shoulders and gently pushed me forward. "He was shot last night."

"His name is Andrés Serrano," I murmured. "He's eighteen. We're from Chihuahua."

"I wouldn't know," he said. "I'm not the registrar. You'll have to leave."

"Can we talk to the registrar? Or is there a list of patients we can check?" Señora Ava asked.

"No, and no. As I said, I can't help you and you can't go in."

As we walked away, he shouted, "You can check at the Servicio Médico Forense mortuary on Chapultepec Avenue if he's dead. If he's not there, try Campo Militar Numero Uno. They're taking the bodies there to identify them… or you could even try the Panteón Civil de Dolores cemetery as a last resort."

I heard his barked instructions even though I jammed my hands over my ears.

His words sparked a terrifying burst of fear and foreboding deep within me, coupled with overpowering rage that rocked me to the core.

I stopped, spun around and glared at him, speechless and shaking.

"*Cállate! Eres un bastardo cruel e insensible.* Shut up! You cruel and callous bastard," Señora Ava shouted. "*Tu desperdicio de espacio sin cerebro!* You brainless waste of space!"

She placed a protective arm around my shoulder. "Take no notice, *cariño*. He doesn't know what he's saying."

Her violent reaction calmed me, though my heart still raced unbearably as we drove back across the suburb to the Chihuahua building.

We found it cordoned off.

Soldiers and granaderos surrounding it waved us on. They refused to allow us to park.

As we drove past, I glimpsed civilians crammed into the backs of three army trucks in the car park behind the building. Most were young students clearly in shock, some without shirts, some with bloodied faces, others being herded by granaderos towards the vehicles at bayonet point. I assumed they'd been arrested hiding in the apartments.

We had to wait at one point to allow a garbage truck to drive slowly off the plaza. Several stiff-fibred street brooms were clipped to its sides. The fogged-up windows of the driver's cabin were closed as powerful jets of water showered over it from tankers parked on each side of the laneway. The spray was washing away the blood and gore splattered along the chassis.

Beyond it on the plaza, I caught sight of a gang of street cleaners working frantically. Partly obscured by sunlight flashing from the wet flagstones, they were hosing down and scrubbing the paving clean of blood and debris.

Back at the house, Señora Carmen had spread a batch of the latest newspapers across the table. She was cutting out articles related to the massacre as Ava searched through the telephone directory for Tío Guillermo's number.

"Take a look at these, Ava," she said, adding without looking up, "and you, Alicia."

Then she puzzled me when she said that every headline reflected the influence and control the president and his PRI party had over the press.

Although she was talking to Ava, I was pleased she'd included me in her invitation, treating me as if I was an adult.

"Not to mention the radio and television stations," she added bitterly. "They're censoring everything. Laundering the information reaching us. Especially with the Olympics so close and the eyes of the world on us."

She slid the cuttings she'd completed across to me.

"Just take a look, Alicia."

She turned back to concentrate on the newspaper she was working on.

I glanced through the cuttings.

The headline for *El Sol* read, '*Barrío el ejército con un foco de subverción en Tlatelolco*', 'The army has averted subversive activities in Tlatelolco'. The *Novedades* was headlined, '*El ejército mantiene tranquilidad y se informa oficial mente de 29 muertos*', 'The army maintains calm and reports an official count of 29 dead'. The *Excélsior* reported the Presidential Press Secretary had declared, '*20 muertos, 75 heridos y 400 presos*' '20 dead, 75 wounded and 400 arrested'.

"You see what I mean?" Señora Carmen said when I'd read through them. "It's false news. They're lying about how many died. They cleaned up the plaza during the night and removed the bodies. We may never know how many were killed."

"They are still cleaning up. We saw them when we drove past," I said.

"The editorials are suggesting the massacre was the result of Cuban communists and Chinese Maoist agents infiltrating the student movement. Look at this example."

She cut out the next paragraph with her scissors and slid it across.

It was taken from *La Prensa.*

I read the headline: *Terroristas Extranjeros*! 'Foreign Terrorists!' And below it, in smaller print, '*Armas de alto poder se utilizaron contra las tropas*', 'High-powered weapons used against the troops'.

She took the cutting back, then raised her pencilled eyebrows. She gave me a bird-like glance as she explained that according to the government's so-called official reports, the communist agents among the students had started the shooting.

"They're telling us the foreigners among the students posted snipers in the Chihuahua building and on the church roof. According to them, they started firing at the soldiers. The army retaliated and the president is taking credit for a job well done. He thinks he's confirmed Mexico's reputation as a stable modern nation by crushing the demonstrators. He believes that might is right and the means justify the end. What nonsense!"

"Communist agents?" I asked. "Is it true? My brother Andrés says it's not."

"Of course it's not."

"Why do they think the students used snipers to shoot the soldiers?" I asked.

I can see the poor officer with the microphone sliding down the wall in front of the photography shop, I thought, shivering as the memory went through my mind.

"It definitely wasn't the students. I suspect a conspiracy. I think it was planned at the highest level. The shootings were carried out by the Olympic Battalion and they used the army as a pawn."

I frowned at her. "What do you mean as a pawn? Like in a game of chess?"

"The first shots came from the top floor of the Foreign Affairs Office tower. Ava and I saw flashes. So did the first two red flares. Students don't have access up there, let alone the roof of the church."

"But why shoot their own soldiers?" I asked again.

"To get the army to respond in the worst possible way. Which they did."

"I took a lot of photographs when it started," I said breathlessly. "And I saw the gunfire too. It came from windows in the Chihuahua building when the lights went out."

Her eyes lit up. "You took *photos*? You did? Where's your camera?"

"I hid it. On one of the pyramids."

"In the rain? It will have ruined the film"

"No, it's in its case. Under a rock."

"You have to find it. You must. Your pictures, they'll be so important."

She gripped my hand, squeezing it as she spoke.

"Listen to me, Alicia. Whatever you do, don't give the film to anyone you don't know for developing. Use someone you trust or do it yourself. I'm sure your papá and tío will understand."

Then Señora Ava called me over to the phone. "It's your Tía Sofia. She has your Papá's number at the university."

2

When Papá arrived, he told us Tío Guillermo had rescued Andrés.

In the confusion, the soldiers at the exit had seen his left hand wrapped in the white handkerchief and waved him through to the car park. They mistook him for a white-gloved member of the Olympic Battalion dealing with a student he'd arrested.

He'd driven to the hospital, where Andrés was now receiving treatment in intensive care, with countless others.

"Andrés was conscious and under sedation when I saw him, but he has suffered. He came round in agony on the back seat of Tío Guillermo's car."

"In agony?"

"In agony. He must have been so sick with shock he could barely endure the pain. He says it was the worst he's ever experienced, but one thought had run through his mind—he had to survive. He had to stay alive, even though there were moments when it was so unbearable he hoped to pass out."

The searing pain he experienced with every bump and vibration struck through him so fiercely he couldn't control his screams, Papá explained.

"He said it was without doubt the worst twenty minutes of his life. But you know our Andrés. When he described how bad the torture was, he joked that at least Tío Guillermo didn't need a siren. Everyone heard them coming. He's in reasonable spirits now, even though the damage to his leg is extensive. The chances of saving it could go either way. He may need an amputation."

"Oh, no. *No! No! No!*"

"He may. We aren't sure yet."

"If he does, will he ever run again?"

I couldn't bear the idea of him on crutches or confined to a wheelchair.

"Run? Who knows? But walk? Yes, I'm sure. With crutches, they told me, and later with a prosthetic if he has an amputation. We can only wait and see."

We returned to Tío Guillermo's unit in the late afternoon. Tía Sofia told us the granaderos and police had released the Chihuahua building from lockdown after they'd entered and ransacked all the units. The power and water supplies were on again.

Just after sundown, Papá and I recovered the camera from the pyramid.

I was relieved to find it where I'd left it. It seemed to be undamaged, though the case was stained with what I feared at first might be blood. Tío Guillermo had handled it and placed it on the ground between Andrés and the dead schoolboy after all—but it proved to be water.

Papá wound the film to the end and extracted it.

By mid-morning the next day, we were examining the twenty-four enlarged colour photographs he had personally overseen being developed in the UNAM graphics laboratory darkroom.

He had arranged for all of them to be printed.

Two negatives were out of focus—the shot of the seller of songbirds I'd taken from high up in the unit and the portrait recording Tío's disapproving expression when we'd first joined the crowd.

Tío Guillermo gave a snort of laughter as he tore the photo up and threw the negative in the waste bin. "We don't need that," he said. "We can do without the photo of a handsome man like me being mistaken for *el Coco*, the Bogeyman."

Then Papá spread them out across the table and examined each in turn. He sorted them in the order of what he considered their dramatic impact.

"This one is without doubt the most sensational."

He placed it face up on the table.

It showed the sharply focused pregnant woman crawling helplessly centre-stage, frozen in the beam of the helicopter spotlight. She was staring directly at the camera. The upturned black pram was behind her. Her mouth was gaping, and her eyes were filled with horror. The body of the schoolboy with wings of blood lay outstretched in the foreground and there were shadows of soldiers advancing across the plaza in the background.

Then he picked it up again and examined it more closely.

"What on earth are they?" he asked. He pointed at five metallic-blue shadows flying high across the cone of light. "Swallow-tailed butterflies? Moths? Surely not. Not during the night."

"Are they bats?" I asked.

"No, they're songbirds," Tío Guillermo replied, peering over his shoulder. "Slate-coloured solitaire thrushes, by the look of them. See the long tails?"

"Oh no," I groaned. "They must have killed the pajarero."

Papá looked at me, before peering back at the photograph. "I don't see any broken cages."

"They must have been smashed in the stampede and cleaned up this morning," Tío Guillermo suggested.

Papá next selected an earlier shot of the same woman standing attentively beside the pram before the shooting. Her two little girls squatted next to her with their hands entangled in the cat's cradle, one with her pink tongue sticking out at the camera. They were framed on the left by the Tepehuán Indian shuffling aside for me. His fellow schoolboy with blond hair was standing in profile on the right. He was glancing sideways with his mouth open, as though protesting that the Indian had shoved him aside to make room for me.

My heart sank as a rush of painful guilt tore me apart. *Such a change in fortune for him with the slight shift in his position because I wanted to take photographs.*

Papá peered down at the two photos for a long time.

He leaned across the table on his outstretched arms before he stood upright, crossed his arms and expired a whistling breath.

"My God, I'm back in Barcelona thirty years ago."

"Why so?" Tío Guillermo asked.

"It's like I'm with Papá Xavier when he showed Mamá and me his photographs of Guernica taken with the same camera." He tapped each photo in turn. "*Antes y después*, before and after. The only difference? His were black and white."

He picked each photo up in turn. '

"Tlatelolco before and Tlatelolco after."

Tío Guillermo nodded. "You wouldn't read about it."

Papá glanced sharply across at him, frowning. "No, no. You would, if someone wrote about it. We're looking at our history here. This is a decisive moment, a watershed in the story of Mexico. *Una segunda Noche Triste*, a second Night of Sorrow."

Tío Guillermo stared knowingly at him. "And I'm looking at the author, who's just thought of the perfect title for his book and has selected the ideal pictures for the front cover."

Papá gathered the photographs together and replaced them in the manila folder, before asking drily, "Where do you suggest we start? With Porfirio Díaz and his overthrow in the revolution in 1910? Or with Lázaro Cárdenas and his reforms in the late 1930s? We both knew him personally when we were kids, after all."

"We swam in his swimming pool."

"Enjoyed his wife's food."

"And rode his horses. What more do you need?"

"You're right," Papá cupped my face in his hands. "Young *mijita* here, with her abu's camera—and poor Andrés, with his new-found activism—are sending me on an important mission to record the outrage and grief we all feel at last night's murderous attack."

"Never to be forgotten," Tío Guillermo's said bluntly. "Those photos record not only the facts, Víctor, they represent our collective revulsion at the shameful bloodshed. They symbolise the outpouring of our deepest emotions. You must publish them. You must. We're all witnesses."

Another tense silence followed before Papá nodded and held up the manila folder.

"One thing's for certain, Díaz Ordaz and the PRI have given up the moral high ground and any political legitimacy with this obscene act of violence."

"They'll lose the support of the middle classes and the intelligentsia. It'll be interesting to see how our writers like Octavio Paz and Carlos Fuentes react, let alone Elena Poniatowska and all the others."

"Not to mention the rest of the world." Papá frowned, placed the folder on the table and struck it repeatedly with a forefinger as he spoke. "The massacre could be just the start."

"Of what?"

"Of a movement leading to full democratisation."

Tío Guillermo gave a burst of cynical laughter. "Good luck with that. The phoenix of democracy rising from the Tlatelolco ashes? You'll need several lifetimes."

"However long it takes."

"Don't hold your breath. Mind you, you could be right. Your experience in extracting precious metals equips you well for digging out the truth."

"If there's any to be found"

"I'm sure you'll find it, even though it may be rare these days."

3

The doctors did not allow me to visit Andrés for four days, but I accompanied Papá and sat in the hospital café while I waited for him.

I did the schoolwork I'd been assigned, read books I'd selected from Papá's collection, or, when I got bored, practised the latest chess moves Papá had taught me on the miniature travelling chess set Abu Cerrildo carved for me—dark brown Aztec warriors on one side, white Spanish conquistadors on the other.

I sat at the same table each day with a view over the courtyard.

A bar of sunlight widening across a line of potted ferns kept me abreast of the time, as the satin greens of their prolific leaves steadily brightened.

After midday, when the sun slanted across the chessboard or the open pages of my book, I'd order another Lulú soda and lunch, before moving to the next table in the shade.

Papá joined me there before we headed home.

I had time to read Mamá's precious battered copy of *The Little Prince* twice and worked my way through a primary school version of *Yolanda Learns to Speak Nahuatl*, which Señora Ava lent me.

On the fourth day, I struggled through the first part of Carlos Castaneda's *The Teachings of Don Juan: A Yaqui Way of Knowledge*. Papá was reading it at the time. Attracted by the thought I'd gain an insight into the Sonoran Yaqui Indian language and culture, I'd snuck it into my satchel without him knowing.

I was learning about the mysterious effects of the playful spirit Mescalito in the peyote leaf on anyone who chewed it or drank the juice and imagining myself communing with lizards foreseeing the future and flying after smoking the

Devil's weed, when Papá appeared and sat down. He had a fit when he saw the book, before roaring with laughter. He snatched it from me. Faces at other tables turned in our direction and smiled when he showed them the cover.

"It's all a fiction," he assured me. "The shaman Don Juan Matus does not exist."

Late that afternoon, we joined Andrés in the ambulance as the paramedics transferred him to the Dr Eduardo Liceaga Hospital, the General Hospital of Mexico City, for his amputation.

"Why can't they save his foot?" I'd asked Papá, when he first gave me the news.

"He's too badly injured," he'd explained, "He has open fractures of the tibia and fibula."

A crushing burst of shock and deep despair overcame me as he explained that fragments of the high-velocity bullet were still lodged in the torn ligaments, bone and tendons. The risk of infection was very high. Blood clots were developing in the lower femoral artery, and he was losing sensation in the limb.

"The surgeons have told me repair is out of the question. Even if they can fix it, the chances are his foot will never function as it should. And the pain is severe at times, but Andrés has been remarkable. He understands and accepts the situation. He says it will be a relief to no longer experience such pain each time the sedatives wear off."

I will never forget the drive.

It was a Sunday, and the church bells rang for evening vespers as we drove across the city. It felt as if we were riding with Andrés to his doom. Holding his hand in the back of the ambulance, I couldn't speak.

I could barely see him at first, his face blurred as tears slid down my cheeks.

"Relax, *mi pequeña cabra*," were his first words to me. His face was pale and his eyes large and glassy, their pupils dilated. "Anyone would think it was you having your foot cut off."

Me having my foot cut off?

I leaned forward, my body shuddering, and grasped his hand in both of mine. I held it to my forehead as if begging his forgiveness for indirectly causing such an unimaginable change in his life.

"I wish it *was* me instead of you," I managed to whisper.

He stroked my hair as we pulled into the hospital driveway. "No, no. You mustn't pity me. Look at it this way, I dodged the other bullet. I'm the luckiest man alive."

My eyes brimmed as I fought to hold my composure. His innocent comment reminded me of the prostrate blond schoolboy lying next to him, the memory so vivid I felt sick.

"Come on, I need you to be strong," he went on quietly. "As strong as you've always been for me. You must help me through this."

Sobbing, I lifted my face close to his.

He put his cheek to mine, and when the rear doors opened, my tears gleamed on his skin and in his sparse beard, before I realised he was crying too.

A jolt of shock tore through me.

When was the last time I witnessed that? Can I ever make it up to him? And if so, how?

"Give me a smile to remember," he said, as the hospital orderlies lifted him out and onto the gurney, "like you usually do. One with my name on it."

He glanced at me for a tense moment, his eyes wide and glistening.

"Ah, that's more like it. *That* is the Alicia I need around me."

He lay back as they wheeled him away.

He needs me? My adored brother Andrés, who's been dealt a hand of winning cards until now, when my insistence on him joining me at the demonstration brought him such misfortune, now he needs me?

I don't think he had any idea how confused I was, how close to impossible it had been to keep my fear and guilt in check and respond with a self-conscious half-smile to his coaxing.

Or does he? I wondered. *And it's his way of calming me down.*

I turned and clung to Papá as Andrés disappeared through the double doors of the emergency entrance. Papá hugged me for several minutes before I choked back my sobs and broke away.

I watched him push open the hospital doors and when I followed him in, I stifled the dread flooding through me.

Early the next afternoon, Papá and I were allowed to visit Andrés in the intensive care unit.

It was a blazing hot Monday, the start of a week that seemed never-ending.

The opening ceremony for the Olympics was due to take place on Saturday, 12 October.

It was so close and yet so far. Like an end-of-year school vacation that can't come soon enough. Or a longed-for birthday circled on a calendar, preceded by countless dates that never reduce even though you cross them out.

I sat in the car squinting against the glare as we crossed the city. I focussed the camera and pretended to take shots of the colourful streets and passers-by, wishing time would pass more quickly, and working out how I'd fill the intervening days.

I was conscious that impatience made time drag more slowly, but couldn't curb my excitement.

It was a relief to come in out of the stifling heat.

I skipped ahead of Papá down the long, whitewashed corridor on the third floor, beneath a row of spinning fans. I followed the six-inch green line painted on the floor leading to the swing doors of the ICU. I made sure my sandalled feet landed squarely on it and didn't touch the forbidding minefield of the ochre tiles on either side.

I waited for Papá at the door.

I was edgy with eagerness.

I peered on tiptoe through the frosted glass window in the door at the shadows of the outstretched patients. Distorted swirling figures in white and green weaved among them as though they were underwater ghosts.

"Settle down, *muñequita*," Papá said when he reached me, placing a restraining hand on my shoulder. "I've warned you. We don't know how he'll be feeling. We have to be prepared."

"I know, but it's Andrés. Won't he be alright?"

"I hope so, but it's a lot for him to take in. And he'll be sedated against the pain." He looked down at me before pushing the door open. "We'll let him do the talking shall we? If he can."

We took our bearings as we entered and saw Andrés lying opposite us across the ward.

His eyes were closed, his face grey and sallow, a clear drip feeding into the back of his right wrist.

I thought he was asleep.

He was leaning back against pillows arranged around him as though he was in an extended armchair. An intricately crocheted white cotton blanket lay across his body. His left leg was encased in what looked like elasticised bandages from his thigh to his foreshortened calf. It was raised in a bedside sling, splints on each side of his knee holding it rigid.

I stared at him, appalled to see him so helpless, so wounded.

When his eyes flashed open his enormous pupils were black and glazed. It took him a moment to focus. He tried to smile, a momentary flicker at the corner of his lips when he recognised me, before lurching away and holding his right hand out to Papá.

For several minutes no words passed between them.

He did not look back at me.

When he closed his eyes again, silent tears slid down beside his nose into his beard.

It triggered a series of unstoppable sobs rising from deep within me.

Bent over, I turned and ran gasping for the door. I burst into the corridor and slid down against the wall. I sat there with my head between my raised knees, my body shuddering. I gave out several agonised howls before taking deep convulsive breaths for self-control, my outpouring prompted as much by fury burning deep within me as despair.

Moments later, a laboratory technician appeared, pushing a two-tiered trolley loaded with rattling phials and instruments.

She stopped beside me.

I didn't look up.

I gazed at her sandals encased in blue plastic overshoes.

"*Estás bien?* Are you alright?" she asked.

When she saw I was unable to reply, she squatted in front of me. She tore several sheets from a roll of paper towels on the lower shelf of her trolley and handed them to me.

"*Déjame traerte un trago de agua,* let me get you a drink of water."

I shook my head and managed to stammer, "Thank you, but no, I'll follow you in."

She steadied me as I staggered to my feet. "*No te apresures. Entra cuando estés lista,* don't rush. Come in when you're ready."

I stood uncertainly at the door for several minutes after she'd disappeared.

When I was about to enter, Papá appeared and held out his arm to stop me. With a hand on the small of my back, he guided me down the corridor away from the ICU. He strengthened his grip when I struggled to break free and run back to Andrés.

"Let me go, Papá. I haven't said goodbye."

"You can't."

"Why not?"

"I was asked to leave. They're preparing to transfer him to the orthopaedic ward."

"So soon?"

"His surgery went well enough for them to move him. They need his bed for another urgent case."

"That's good, isn't it?"

"I'm sure it is."

When we stopped beside the lifts, he led me to a wooden bench beneath the window. He patted the slats to his right.

"Listen to me, *mijita*, we believe you should stay away until he's well on the way to recovery."

I sat beside him, stunned. "*We?* Doesn't Andrés want to see me?"

"You know he does, but not right now. By us I mean the doctors and me. It doesn't do him any good to see you so upset."

"I couldn't help it."

"I know."

"It just happened." Helpless, and for a moment feeling unwanted, I stiffened in a burst of fury at the unfairness of it.

"I know, and so does he."

"I won't do it again," I snapped.

"I'm sure you'll try not to."

"I won't. I just *won't.*"

"Look, he has a lot to deal with. You're aware of that. His life has been disrupted. He must start again. With everything. He must learn to adjust. Simple things to start with." He held out a fist and extended a finger in turn, "Like getting out of bed and dressing, eating and drinking, sleeping… even breathing, I suspect. He's exhausted after the surgery and full of different drugs. You saw the way he looked."

"He looked terrible. And when I saw him crying…"

"He's in shock and he's confused."

"So am I."

"I know, I know." He put an arm around my shoulder and pulled me to his side. "I'm going to arrange counselling for you when we're home. There's one thing you must be clear about—it was not your fault. None of us knew what was going to happen."

"But if it hadn't been for me—"

"No, no. You're not to blame, not in any way. You were interested in the crowds and curious about the demonstration. Besides, you wanted to use the camera. It's natural for someone your age. I'd have done the same when I was young." He leaned forward and looked into my eyes. "It was a nasty coincidence, an unfortunate chance accident, you understand?"

"An accident?"

"Yes."

Despite his words, dreadful feelings of self-blame flooded my mind, as they had when Tía Ariché had told me about Mamá. I shook my head to dismiss the overpowering sensation.

"I can't bear to think of Andrés never running again. Never *ever*," I said. "Not the way he does now."

But I will, the sudden determined thought arose. *I'll keep running for him. For both of us. And for Mamá, as we did in Urique Cemetery.* At precisely the same moment stunning doubts flashed across my mind. *Only for as long as I enjoy it.*

I have neither the desire nor the talent to succeed at world-class level that Andrés does. They are his dreams, not mine.

"Look, we don't know what the future holds," I heard Papá continue. "Right now, he's about to experience a hurricane of different emotions as he comes to terms with what's happened."

"We can help him, can't we?"

"Yes, we can. We can encourage him. And support him. But it's up to him. He has to realise what's happened and acknowledge the extent of it. There's no going back. His life will be different. He must learn what he can do and not get depressed by what he can't. Too much grieving won't be good for him." He took a deep breath and sighed. "Or anger. Or depression. It's going to take him some considerable time before he accepts the situation." He tapped his temple with a forefinger. "In here." He placed his hand over his heart and bent to clutch his left ankle. "As well as in here... and down here."

"How long will that take?"

"It all depends."

"What about you? You'll visit him, won't you?"

"I will, as often as visitors are allowed." He took my left hand in his and lifted it to his lips, briefly kissing my fingers. "As for you, *mijita*, you can go to the Games with Tía Sofia on the days we have the tickets for and watch the rest of the events on her colour television. Tío Guillermo and I will come with you when we can, at least for part of the time. You can take the camera."

"I'll take the best photographs I can to show Andrés when he's ready to see me."

"I know you will. He's sure to appreciate them."

He withdrew his arm from around my shoulder and leaned forward with both hands on the bench as he prepared to stand. I put my hand on his chest. "Just one thing, Papá.

If Andrés can't go to the Games, why should I? Won't it upset him? It seems so unfair."

He sat back and patted my knee. "Don't overthink the situation, *mijita*. He's just as likely to be upset if you don't go. It's what you both came here to do, so do it for him." He raised his eyebrows and gave me an appreciative glance. "I'm pleased you care so much you're putting yourself in Andrés's shoes to understand how he'd feel about you going without him, but I'm sure he'd feel far worse if it prevented you from doing so. So go. Enjoy it. Without a second thought." He stood and pulled me upright. "And let's hear no more about it."

We were the only two descending in the lift when he turned to face me.

He gave me a long, searching look, and with both hands on my shoulders, applied some downward pressure. "Don't let Andrés's troubles weigh you down, *cariño*. When you take your photographs, take them for him." He released his hands, cupped my face, and then surprised me when his next words echoed my recent thoughts. "And when you run in future, why don't you run for both of you? Until the day comes when he can run for himself."

"He will?"

"I wouldn't say it if I didn't believe it." I looked up at him as he nodded, as if he was certain about something I now so strongly doubted. "*Siento en mis huesos*, I feel in in my bones."

About to contradict him, I stiffened and did not reply as unexpected thoughts raced through my mind. Andrés was ten years older than me and had been a hero to me since I was young. I held him in awe and had become his running shadow, often much to his annoyance. We both shared the tragedy of losing Mamá at an early age and running cemented our closeness more strongly than we acknowledged, especially since he was able to bring her to life for me as we ran more realistically than I could in my imagination—as he had in the cemetery last year.

When we stepped into the foyer, Papá withdrew a small brown envelope from his back pocket and handed it to me. "I think you're responsible enough to look after these."

I lifted the flap and emptied eight tickets to the *Estadio Olimpico Universitario*, the Olympic Stadium, into the palm of my right hand.

I stared down at them, speechless, before fanning them out with a scream of delight.

They were blue with a yellow band through the centre, four dated 'Tuesday 15 Oct' and four for the next day.

They all showed the icon of a running shoe for athletics, an archway with the number three, indicating our entrance gate, seated figures and the numbers 31135–31138. Two symbolic clocks indicated our entry and departure times—eleven and five o'clock. On the back was a graphic oval showing the seating in the stadium. A small red arrow indicated our seats were on the second tier next to the rail, partway down the home straight.

I raised my arms above my head, tickets in one hand, envelope in the other, spun around Papá several times and tore out into the glaring afternoon sunlight when he opened the door for me. Breathless and jubilant, I gave him an energetic long-lasting hug.

"Better not lose them. Guard them with your life."

"Trust me, Papá, I will. With my life. I can't wait!"

I woke up while it was still dark on Saturday morning, immediately alert and bursting with anticipation.

Without waking Papá, I put on my trapeze dress and tiptoed into the lounge. I switched on Tía Sofia's colour TV and, with the sound muted, watched the build-up to the opening ceremony.

They were showing a repeat of the arrival of the Olympic torch at Veracruz six days ago. Seventeen swimmers in a relay were side stroking from the cruiser *Durango*, each holding a torch in the air and lighting the next torch in sequence until the flame reached the shore.

The swim was interrupted by a brief flashback I hadn't seen before.

It showed the moment the torch had arrived a week earlier in the Bahamas, at the place where Cristobal Colon—Christopher Columbus—had landed, coincidentally on 12 October 1492, on the island of Guanahaní.

I knew he had renamed the island San Salvador.

The flame was used to light a cauldron modelled on an Aztec brazier dedicated to the fertility goddess of corn, Xilonen. It sat on a pedestal in the town's plaza.

I was amazed when the commentator mentioned the original brazier on which the replica was modelled had been dug from from a pyramid in Tlatelolco years before.

A rush of excitement raced through me. *From the same pyramid where I hid my camera? From the same crevice? It must be. It just has to be!*

I followed the journey of the flame from Veracruz through towns and cities in the south-east. It ended up in the late evening on an upper tier of the Pyramid of the Moon in Teotihuacan, where a spectacular Aztec ceremony of the New Fire was performed. It was the first, the commentator said, since it was last performed by Montezuma in 1507.

The opening ceremony was underway when Tía Sofia appeared.

She opened the curtains, allowing shafts of sunlight to pour across the room. She switched up the sound and settled cross-legged beside me on the carpet.

She put an arm around my shoulders.

"I should have known you'd be up. Did you get any sleep?"

"Enough, thank you. I can't wait for the Games to start."

"No! I'd never have guessed." She gave me a teasing smile. "Are you hungry?"

"A little. What are we having?"

"Quick and easy *molletes*. Something you can eat in front of the TV without being distracted."

"Oh, yum."

"Would you like bacon topping with yours? Or tomato and jalopeños? Or all three?"

"All three, please. Can I help?"

"You stay where you are and give me a running commentary. I'll start with coffees for the two snoring señores.'"

By mid-morning, the Olympic stadium was packed to overflowing when President Díaz Ordaz and a group of dignitaries arrived.

They took their seats to a twenty-one-gun salute, a fanfare of trumpets and the singing of the national anthem. Five colourful gigantic balloons representing the Olympic rings floated skywards, and the athletes appeared in their multicoloured uniforms, marching in time and in disciplined rows and columns into the stadium to the regular drumbeat of a military band.

They circled the stadium and took their places on the grass in the centre.

The formality of the athletes surprised me.

I gave a burst of laughter each time I saw someone skip getting back into step. When Tía Sofia asked what had amused me, I explained I often did the same at school, but for the opposite reason—to be the only one deliberately *out* of step.

When the president's voice rang out, declaring the Games open, and the Olympic flag was raised, a rush of anger rose like bile in my throat. I switched off the sound and glanced away. I couldn't bear hearing his voice or looking at him as he spoke. The thought of Andrés lying helpless on the plaza below and now in the hospital bed was unbearable.

I switched the sound back on when the mayors of Tokyo and Mexico City exchanged another smaller Olympic flag on a pole. Tía Sofia explained that it was the Antwerp flag, first handed across in the 1920 ceremony in the city of that name.

"I've been reading about it," she said. "I thought I'd show some interest, even though I'm not a sporty person, especially now the Games are going ahead here. Guillermo was worried they'd be transferred to Los Angeles."

The wind was up, and the flag wrapped itself around the head of the guardsman carrying it, blinding him. He had to feel his way up the six steps onto the pink dais. Applause rang out when he didn't trip over. He untangled himself and handed the flag across, the band playing '*La Zandunga*', an Andalusian waltz. I recognized it after a few bars—Andrés had recently been mastering it on his guitar following Papá's instructions, and I'd been unsuccessfully following him in the background.

At the same time, an astonishing cloud of multicoloured balloons was released.

"Do you know how many there are?" Tía Sofia asked.

"Ten thousand?"

"More."

"Twenty?"

"Twice that. Forty thousand of them."

"Wow! I'm glad I didn't have to blow them up."

I held my breath as the torchbearer appeared to a fanfare

of drums, conch shells and reed flutes—and then I recognized her.

"Tía Sofia, it's Queta Basilio," I squealed. "They've chosen a woman to light the cauldron! She's our hurdles champion. I saw her on TV at the Olympic trials."

Dressed in white, her black hair tied back with a white sash and holding the torch high in her right hand, she circled the track in an anticlockwise direction, before mounting the steps to the cauldron in the back straight. She looked fit and strong as she bounded effortlessly up the stairway that I'd imagined climbing during Andrés's race. At the top, she turned, held the torch high and out towards the athletes, before lighting the cauldron. The flame erupted and the crowd roared.

The athletes' oaths were read, the national anthem played again, an enormous flock of pigeons was released, and the Games were underway.

Ten days later, with the Games still in progress, I upended the envelope and tipped all the photographs I'd taken across an open space on Andrés's bed.

He watched me with a patient amused look, his hands behind his head, his latest plaster cast raised on a pillow.

His calmness surprised and pleased me, but I wondered how he was feeling deep down after his second operation. Papá had told me the surgeons had removed a further section of bone from below the knee when unexpected complications had set in after the first amputation.

Looking back on it now, I believe the painkillers had numbed him and the extent to which the trajectory of his life had altered had not yet sunk in.

I busied myself by concentrating on sorting the photographs into as close to their calendar sequence as I could remember.

The first was the shot Andrés had taken of me in the parking lot of the athletes' village, sitting on the metal sculpture of the Mexico 1968 logo. I was about to bite into the grilled corn *elote*. I pointed at three African athletes walking past in their army-green tracksuits, "Ethiopia" imprinted on the back.

I tapped my forefinger on the athlete looking across at me. I hadn't noticed him at the time the photo was taken.

"Can you guess who this is?" I asked.

He picked up the photo and peered at it, without looking up.

"It's got to be Mamo Wolde, second in my race, the ten thousand metres. My God, what a runner. I've seen the replays again and again. Him and the Kenyan I trained with, Naftali Temu, battling around the last lap and down the final straight, Wolde leading until the last fifty metres when Temu sprinted past. I told you the Kenyans had an extra gear and overdrive."

"They were followed by Gammoudi, weren't they?" I asked, pleased I'd remembered the name, especially since Andrés had mentioned him to me before. "Didn't he come third?"

"Yes, and then our Juan Martinez, who led for most of the last five laps, as I warned the Kenyans." He gave a sympathetic pursing of his lips, "The Australian, Ron Clarke, followed them home in sixth."

"At least he finished. I remember you said he may not, may even have *died* because of the altitude." I hesitated, unsure whether I should have referred to the dangers associated with the Games because of the altitude, before changing the subject with a question. "What was Naftali's time again?"

"Twenty-nine minutes, twenty-seven seconds or so."

"And yours at the trial?" I asked, before looking up at him and flinching when I realised how insensitive the question was.

I held my breath before he replied.

"Don't remind me. Thirty minutes forty-eight point four seconds, according to Abu Cerrildo. A second slower by the official timekeeper."

"I prefer Abu's stopwatch."

"So do I, even if it puts me a lap behind at the end."

He looked down at the photo and shook his head.

"It's hard to realise I'll never have my time recorded in my favourite race as an able-bodied athlete again."

I felt as if he'd slapped me hard across the cheek.

I had no reply, so I reached for the next photo.

"I managed to get this one for you," I said breathlessly. "Tía Sofia took me to the athletes' village. We spoke to Kimaru Songok. He remembers you. So do some of the other Kenyans. He arranged for us to meet Naftali, and I took this shot of him. I took the print back to him the other day to get him to sign it for you."

I handed him the photograph.

Naftali was standing in the plaza wearing his red tracksuit and barefoot, the gold medal around his neck. He'd printed a message across it—'*Kwa* Andres, *bahati nzuri na maisha yako ya baadaye*' and signed it '*Rafiki yako*, Naftali Temu.'

I saw Andrés wince and frown before he flicked the photo back on the bed, face-up.

I pointed at the inscription. "It's Swahili. It says, 'For Andrés, good luck with your future, your friend, Naftali Temu.' Kimaru translated it for me."

I gave him a shy half-smile, hoping to lighten the mood.

"He forgot the accent on the *e* in your name."

"Thank you, but I don't know whether to laugh or cry."

He held my hand for a moment. His palm was dry and hot.

"You know how it is when you've just been given something brand new? A bike or a new pair of shoes? And you spend the next six months looking for every bike or pair of shoes of the same make you never noticed before? Well, that's me right now. Every time someone comes in here, I notice they have a whole left leg and mine is missing." He tapped the photo. "It happened when you walked in and when I looked at Naftali just now. He can still run. So can you. I can't."

Stunned, I had no idea how to respond.

"It's hard. It might be different when I get my prosthetic. They've already measured me for one."

"Will it arrive soon?"

"They have no idea. Until then, it's a wheelchair."

He let go of my hand, stretched and put both of his behind his head again.

"I hate to think of myself as disabled. Hate it," he growled, before taking a deep breath. "But guess who's going to be pushing me around?"

The vivid image of me pushing him in his wheelchair along the Conchos River footpath at a fast trot flashed through my mind. "Geronimo?" I suggested, distracting him. "Pulling you from the front using his lead as a harness?"

"Geronimo. Now, there's a thought."

"Do you want to see the rest?" I asked him, to change the subject.

"Sure. Show me what you've got."

We ran through them, beginning with Tuesday's events.

The discus and javelin finals.

The pole vault.

Tall and slender Wyomia Tyus of the USA winning the women's one hundred metres, and the Kenyans, Amos Biwott and Ben Kogo, first and second in the steeplechase, both clearing away down the home straight.

"What about the men's two hundred metres?" he asked. "Did you photograph the finish? It was so close."

"I did. The end of the race and the medal presentation."

I was excited he asked. Papá thought they were the pick of

the photographs and had been full of praise for them.

"The medal presentation? Show me."

I selected the three photos I'd taken, one of the race, two of the presentation.

The first showed black American Tommy Smith bursting smoothly through the tape a fraction ahead of the Australian Peter Norman, with another black American, John Carlos, close behind in third. It was slightly blurred, suggesting the effect of speed.

"You should have heard the spectators at the end of the race," I said. "They were going mad because it was so close, but that was nothing compared to what happened at the medal presentation afterwards. It was late in the afternoon. I had to concentrate on the light and focusing the Leica, so it took me a while looking through the viewfinder as they took their places on the dais. Before taking the shot, I looked up to check the settings. When I looked over at them, I couldn't believe it, Andrés. Tommy Smith and John Carlos weren't wearing shoes. They had their tracksuits rolled up and were both wearing black socks. Here, look for yourself."

"Yes, they are. But look at what else they're doing. You caught it beautifully."

I didn't reply at once as I recalled I'd had to refocus to ensure I captured all the details.

As the Stars and Stripes flag was raised and the Star-Spangled Banner sounded, they lowered their heads. At the same time, they raised a fist wearing a black glove—in the Black Power salute, Papá told me later—Smith's on his right hand and Carlos's on his left. I'd snapped two shots, catching them as they stood with their heads bowed and arms raised, with Peter Norman gazing at the flagstaff.

I remember the spectators around me were shocked into a sudden silence before bursting into deafening jeers and shouts of outrage at the defiant show of obvious disrespect.

While I wasn't aware of the deep political meaning behind their protest, the courage and daring they showed in facing the hostility of the spectators thrilled me, and I blocked out the noise.

"When Papá and I looked closely at the photos yesterday," I said, "we noticed all three of them, including Peter Norman, are wearing those round yellow badges over their hearts. See them? I borrowed Tía Sofia's magnifying glass and read what's printed on them."

"What?" Andrés held up the photo to squint at it. "I can't make it out."

"The 'Olympic Project for Human Rights'. You told me what human rights are, the other day." I reached across and pointed at the photo. "Look at Tommy Smith. He's holding an open brown cardboard box against his left hip. See the green leaves in it? Papá says it must be an olive branch."

Andrés frowned at me and said one of the TV commentators had confirmed they had both broken other forbidden Olympic protocols—in Smith's case by wearing a black scarf around his neck and in Carlos's a beaded necklace visible in the open collar of his tracksuit top.

"He said they were protesting on behalf of the American Black Power organisation. The scarf and black socks represent the poverty many black Americans experience." He looked more closely at the photo. "And Carlos's beads; see them there round his neck? The black ones? They symbolise the estimated two million slaves who died in the ships carrying them to the Americas, following the Middle Passage across the Atlantic. How brilliant!"

"And the *gloves*," I said excitedly. "Papá says they must have shared the same pair. One each. He says it took a lot of courage for them to do what they did. All three of them, even the Australian. He says they'll be remembered for a long time, but it's going to cause them heaps of trouble. The Olympic

Committee won't stand for it."

Andrés thrilled me when he tapped the photo with his forefinger and said, "You don't know what you've done here, *pequeña cabra*. You've captured another moment in history with Abu's camera. Papá can use it in the book he's planning."

He raised his right fist, clenched in a salute.

"Black Power! I told you about it before the Games when the black athletes were considering going on strike, remember? Here it is in action."

He raised it to his lips and gave it a kiss.

"I love it… love it… *love* it."

Andrés running with a prosthetic foot – Courtesy Sportpoint / Alamy stock photo

CHAPTER TEN

1

In Saucillo, Northern Mexico, 1969 – ongoing

THE YEAR 1968 WAS a turning point in my relationship with Andrés.

Three weeks after his surgery, he returned home to Saucillo to recover.

He took leave from his studies.

The evening before his arrival Papá forewarned us we we'd have to be patient and understanding with him. He called Camila and me into the lounge just on sunset. I'd been jogging round the circuit in the back yard, where Abu was carving his latest selenite crystal chess miniatures.

"We're going to have to be very careful with Andrés tomorrow," he said. "It's not just the physical pain he has to put up with. It's learning to do the simple things we take for granted—"

"Like what?" I asked, panting.

"Like moving from the bed to the wheelchair. Using the toilet. Washing and dressing."

"He was already doing all that when we saw him in hospital, wasn't he?"

"He was, and he is becoming self-sufficient; but now he has to learn to be kind to himself. He must give himself time to adjust to the changes. Get used to having no left foot. He has to recover emotionally and come to terms with not being able to run the way he used to."

"That's going to be hard for him."

"Yes, it will. Very difficult."

"What can we do, then?"

"Be patient. Help him whenever he asks you to. Be aware he'll be grieving as he comes to accept the changes. It won't be easy."

Why not? I wondered. *He is Andrés, after all. He's a fighter.*

"He's strong, isn't he?" I asked.

"Of course he is; but think about it. Put yourself in his place. His life's been turned upside down. He'll be angry and depressed. He'll find it hard to accept what's happened to him, let alone come to terms with it and start rebuilding his life. He'll be asking "Why me?" and we'll need to encourage him to keep going. To believe in himself. To find the strength to overcome the hardships he'll have to face. Step by step."

"Will it be as difficult as you say for him?"

"It will. For him—and for you. He's on another journey now, just as he was for the Olympics. A journey to find a new vision for himself. To develop a new mindset as he learns his limitations. And that will affect your relationship with him."

"Él *podría sorprenderos a todos,* He might surprise us all, Señor Victor," Camila said. "*Si el es el Andrés lo conozco.* If he's the Andrés I know,"

"He might."

"No! He *will*," I said fiercely.

Within days I discovered how much Andrés had changed.

The first time I pushed him in his wheelchair for a short walk along the paved section of the Conchos River embankment, I floundered helplessly in a gravelled section where the concrete had broken up.

We were a kilometre from home.

"Look out!" he screamed, as the left wheel dug into the sand.

The wheelchair lurched sideways before swerving so violently the handgrip was torn from my grasp.

He toppled clumsily out, despite my desperate efforts to prevent it.

He saved himself from falling to the ground by clutching an armrest and hopping crazily round the wheelchair on his right leg.

Geronimo rushed around us, barking excitedly, as if we were engaged in some new game.

I was so relieved he hadn't crashed to the ground, and he looked so comical dancing round the upturned chair, I gave out a nervous laugh. I guiltily stifled it when I looked at his red face. I was shocked to see his expression twisted with pain and rage.

"Are you blind?" he screamed. "Look where you're going, you little idiot. You could have torn open the sutures."

On the verge of tears, I helped him right the wheelchair and he levered himself back into it. I adjusted the right footrest for him as he reached forward and gingerly felt the stump through the compression sock.

"I'm in enough pain as it is, without you making things worse," he said, his voice a growl.

"I'm so sorry, Andrés," I said in a strained whisper. "I didn't mean to."

I saw him set his jaw. "Just take care!"

He did not speak to me again on the way home.

I could barely breathe as I pushed him back to the house.

When we kayaked together on the Conchos River later that week, I took his irritable outbursts of frustration at the pain and discomfort he experienced with the seat and positioning of his legs personally, even though he was not directing them at me.

"My God, it's worse than being stabbed in the leg with a knife, Alicia. Multiple times… and the pain at night! I can't sleep. My medications are useless." Then he added in a wild outburst, "This is no way to live! I can understand why some people in my circumstance would rather die."

I suffered unduly as I towed him back to the landing, unable to please or calm him.

My feelings swerved between empathy and distaste.

At least you're alive, the thought kept running across my mind. *You should be grateful for that—and for everything we're doing for you. Stop feeling sorry for yourself.*

Despite Papá's advice I soon ran out of patience.

I found it impossible to tolerate his moodiness.

I had never known him to be so negative and quick to anger, so mean, moody and emotional. So self-absorbed. I knew he was suffering but had no idea how to deal with the changes in his personality as he grappled with losing his Olympic dream and the effects of post-traumatic shock.

My emotions were so mixed I came close to hating him, though I never dared to say so.

I was relieved when he returned to Mexico City a month later, to fit his prosthetic limb and continue with his architectural studies.

He did not return for over a year.

During that time Papá and Abu Cerrildo updated me on his progress.

"He enjoys his studies," Papá told me once when I asked, "and he's doing well at them, but he can't stand his prosthetic foot. He considers its design primitive, and it's only a "stop-gap", as he puts it. It's too stiff. Yes, he can walk on it, but he can't run, and if there's one thing you and I both know about him, running was his life."

"*Is* his life," I corrected him. "I don't think that's changed. It's just frustrating him that he can't."

"I beg your pardon. *Is* his life. So, guess what?"

"I don't know."

"Take a guess."

"Is he going to ask whoever made it to design a better one, maybe? With more flexibility?"

Papá laughed. "Close, but you know Andrés. He's impatient and so determined to run again, he's working on it himself. He asked Abu the other day to dismantle the old wooden rocking horse you kids never play with anymore. You know, the one he made for you with the single leaf of a car spring bouncing it. He wants to use the spring leaf as a foot, somehow."

"How?"

"Who knows? *Está obsesionado...* he's obsessed with the idea."

"Wouldn't it be too heavy? And even stiffer than the foot he's got?"

"You would think so, but let's wait and see what he has in mind. He won't be using the whole leaf, after all. I guess he'll be using part of it and thinning it down."

I had to smile. "If he succeeds, he'll make a great long jumper. Bouncing like a kangaroo."

Papá was right.

When Andrés came home for a week during his long vacation the following July, he'd regained his previous enthusiasm for the idea of running—this time as a Paralympian, assuming the Games would eventually include athletes wearing prosthetics —and his zest for living.

He had changed.

I found it a joyful relief to share his company again.

He spent hours with Abu in the work shed cutting a segment from the curved leaf of the spring, grinding it back and shaping it to the template he had in mind.

"It'll be shaped like the rear leg of a galloping horse, *mi pequeña cabra montañosa*," he explained one afternoon as I watched him working with the grinder. Short-lived showers of sparks were shooting across the workshop. "If you examine it at full gallop closely it curves back and forward like a Spanish inverted question mark."

"Like Abu's scythe he uses on the lawns?"

"Exactly, but flattened where it hits the ground, to give traction."

When he took it back to Mexico City with him, he was still puzzling over how to attach it to his amputated leg.

I enjoyed spending time with him at the dining table each evening watching him work on a project he was due to present for his architectural studies.

I was especially interested when he introduced me to the house designs of the Australian architect Glen Murcutt. He had photocopied several Murcutt houses from articles in architectural magazines held in the Polytechnic Institute library. One had caught his eye—a small, neat wood and corrugated iron farmhouse he thought would be ideal for the Sierra Madre environment. He was redesigning the floor plan and simplifying its structure as part of his project.

"You remember *Janus*, the sculpture I worked on, and you photographed?" he asked me one evening. "I've been trying to contact the sculptor, Clement Meadmore. I don't know if he'll remember me, but I want to ask him if he knows Glen Murcutt. I want to find out if he's published any books with his work in them. If he has, I'll ask him to get one for me. There's no harm in trying." He tapped the picture. "Can you imagine how practical little houses like this would suit our people living on the slopes of the barrancas?"

I look back on that week with some amazement. It was as if the next twenty years of his life were being foretold and about to unroll before us.

After qualifying in 1974, he established an architectural business in Chihuahua City, designing farmhouses throughout the state, and in the Sierra Madre. Then he received an invitation in 1976 from his old coach, Señor Valentin, to join a worldwide team of amputee athletes testing prosthetic equipment being produced by the German Ottobock firm. He'd be acting as their representative in Mexico.

Their aim was to convince the Olympic Committee to allow their ongoing use in the Paralympics after the 1988 Seoul Games.

By 1978, when I was 18, he was running freely again with a refined prosthetic, and he never looked back.

He often hinted that if he was fortunate enough to represent Mexico in a future Paralympic Games, he'd like to use me as a training partner.

"I'm sure the prosthetics will get the green light," he said. "I'll need a training partner, *mi pequeña cabra*, so make sure you keep fit for me. You'll be doing us both a favour."

I told him I would, and I've kept my word.

Alicia contemplating her future – Courtesy Shutterstock

EPILOGUE

IT IS AUGUST 3, 1978. I have just typed the last sentence in our story. I hope you enjoyed reading it as much as I did writing it.

It's a relief to know it's finished.

I can now look out at the Pacific on this beautiful blue-sky day knowing I won't be delving into more of my memories of 1967-8 to record them.

That said, for those of you who may be wondering what happened to me as I grew into my teens, I have decided to include this brief epilogue to being you up to date—much as they do in documentaries, commenting on the afterlives of the principal characters.

Looking back, those years since I was eight years old flew past.

I performed reasonably well at primary school and passed most subjects at secondary school as I matured, excelling in Languages and scraping through in Maths and Science. I strove to succeed, both to win Papá's ongoing approval and to impress on the women in my extended family and the neighbourhood that I was never going to meekly fill the expected role of housewife and mother as they had done.

I decided early on I'd live my life on my own terms. I chose to ignore their frequent warnings I was heading for a fall and their suggestions that if Mamá had lived, she would have been horrified.

"I can't imagine what Suré would have to say about your attitude, Alicia," was a frequent critical refrain I heard from the mothers of girls with whom I shared sleepovers. "You'd be thinking and behaving differently if she'd lived."

Without Mamá's guidance, femininity was the last thing on my mind.

I developed a steely and, I like to think, resilient independence as I adapted to the physical and social changes I faced as I grew up.

What mattered to me was Papá's pride in my progress and the fact that he encouraged me to undertake tertiary studies in Linguistics, starting in a fortnight. He agreed to finance me, allowing me to enjoy the same opportunities as Andrés.

I turned to Tía Ariché and our maid Camila as surrogate mothers when I needed to.

I sought their guidance and comfort when I experienced my first period and needed information in matters of sex; or when I was beset by anxiety in my relationships with girls who hated my attitude and resented my success—and my occasional, always short-lived, crushes on boys. I even described the excitement of my first experimental backyard kiss to Camila.

I'll always be grateful to her for designing and sewing the lime green blouse and flare pants decorated with sequins I wore for my fifteenth birthday, my celebratory coming-of-age *quinceañera*.

"No, I am *not* going to wear one of those," I told her, pointing at the customary lacy and glamorous white and pink ball gowns other fifteen-year-olds selected from, during my fitting at the dressmakers. "Never! If anyone insists, then I won't be attending."

"What will you wear?" she asked.

I rifled through the pantsuits hanging in a display wardrobe and selected a smart green safari suit. "Something like this."

Camila raised her eyebrows and gave out a quiet chuckle. "Only my Alicia," she said quietly. "You won't be the belle of the ball wearing trousers like the men."

"Exactly," I said, "but at least I'll be true to myself."

I scandalised the many guests at the gathering and to this day, haven't heard the end of it. The fact that I reflected my 'personality' in a blouse and flare pants rather than a frilly gown, and did away with the religious ceremony, was seen by many as an unforgivable insult to tradition.

I enjoyed the party, though.

I appreciated the powerful symbolism behind the rites of my initiation into Mexican womanhood.

When the music began, Papá led me to a chair and removed my leather sandals when I extended each leg in turn. He replaced them with a pair of smart black high heels. I'd practised dancing round the tiled kitchen in them for weeks. Then he pulled me up into his arms with an exaggerated flourish and we took to the open floor in the coming-out waltz, before many of the guests joined us.

Later, I exchanged my bunch of flowers for a sceptre at the banquet table and walked away with it at the end of the night—a woman at last, but strictly on my terms. I was simply asserting myself and following tradition as I chose.

I expect to complete my Masters in Linguistics and Applied Linguistics at Guadalajara University in 1983 and hope to spend the next four years at the West Virginia University in Morgantown, completing my PhD studies. I've selected the West Virginia University because Papá has often been invited to speak at geological conferences there, the state being the coal mining capital of the United States.

After that, who knows?

The future beckons.

I'll come to yet another fork in the road and my life may take a sudden, unexpected turn, as it has in the past.

Acknowledgements

Tʜɪs ɴovᴇʟ wouʟᴅɴ'ᴛ ʜᴀvᴇ seen the light of day in its current form without the cooperation and advice of others. This is the first time I've made the leap into YA writing and I was floundering without them. I owe them my deepest thanks.

My perceptive seventeen-year-old granddaughter Kaylee Monaco to start with. She surprised me with the depth and accuracy of her know-how and her enthusiasm. She guided me in aspects of the YA novel writing process I had little clue about. Thank you Kaylee, for your patience and invaluable advice.

Lynne Stringer, my reliable and brilliant editor who has devoted so much time to correcting and tweaking all my work over the years. Lynne's changes are always on the money. They never fail to improve the word choice, plot sequences and storylines. I owe you my heartfelt thanks.

Tireless James Munro of Australian e-book publishing, whose extensive technical skills I have tested many times. Thank you for your creativity in preparing my work for publication to the highest standards and for your persistence and timeliness.

Many thanks also to my pre-publication researchers, readers and advisers whose guidance and interest I value: Mike and Jenny Purchase, Karen and Elly Monaco, Gill Bennett, De Kropach, Bruce and Inka Hutton, Cam and Jae, Jessica Lee, Dayna Norris and Kay Stehn. Without you none of my work would have reached the reading public.

About the Author

Born in Tanzania, from the age of six I was fortunate to grow up in Mombasa on the Kenya coast. One of my goals in life was to research the Arab, Chinese, Portuguese and Dutch explorers who sailed along the East African Swahili coast for centuries.

I migrated to Perth, Western Australia, in 1963. After a 7-year stint as a High School teacher, I transferred to Human Resources and worked on remote mine sites in the Pilbara, Northern Territory and Papua New Guinea. This brought me into close contact with local Indigenous people. I found their culture, deep rooted love of country, resilience and unfailing sense of humour inspirational.

I retired in 2008 and since then have dedicated myself to writing fictional novels based on historical themes. 3 of these comprise the Truth and Reconciliation Trilogy: *The Glass Cenotaph*, *The Life and Times of Gerrit de Waal* and *Alicia*. They draw on 20 years of archival research undertaken in Australia, South Africa and the Netherlands (Zeeland), and an appreciation of Australia's First Nations people, who have survived the effects of European settlement and colonialism. The trilogy gives you a fresh look at Australia's colonial history and reflects the current dialogue between the Aboriginal First Nation people and the rest of Australia.

I have also written two YA novels, *My Brother, Andrés* you've just read, and *The Dreams of Summer Dartson*, and have published a number of short stories, most of them included in the collection *Thank You, Gabe*. Some scenes in all three are drawn from sections of the trilogy. I trust you enjoy reading the novels and short stories as much as I enjoyed writing them.

www.ingramcontent.com/pod-product-compliance
Lightning Source LLC
Chambersburg PA
CBHW070320190726
48291CB00014B/2452